Can You Play MacArthur Park?

W.J. "Duke" Mader

ISBN: 1479249440
ISBN-13: 978-1479249442

DEDICATION

The mantle of success comes in all sizes, colores and fabrics: awards we have won, accomplishments we have achieved, milestones we have reached. I can say with great satisfaction that I have enjoyed a fulfilling life and have achieved the endorsement of three exceptional children: Yvonne, John II, and Christopher*. I couldn't be prouder of these three children. They have honored me with my own special pedestal. In all the world there is not greater joy a parent can know than the love and respect of his children. I dedicate this book to my children and my wife, Zita, who is the engine that makes the train go.

(*Christopher was murdered in 2004.)

BARROOM MADONNA

She is a quiet figure sitting in the corner all alone.
Sipping her drink; remembering the better times she's known.
She knows every song the juke box plays,
Mouthing the words so no one can hear, her eyes agaze.
From across the dark barroom into the quiet of yesterdays past,
Her eyes full with tears, her lonely heart breaking, reliving those thoughts that last.
A man in the night; she won't ask his name,
She never sees their faces, to her they are all the same.
The Madonna of the barroom is a quiet, lonely dame.
The Madonna of the barroom whose only friend is pain.
She is there for us to see of what once was, and what still could be.
"You see," she said, "my world has died. There's no one left but me."
She's quiet as a shadow fading with the morning light.
Not to be seen again until the guilt of night.
This Madonna of the barroom,
A story of a woman---out of grace and out of glory.
Feels this Madonna of the barroom, not remorse not pity, just sorry.

By: W. J. Duke Mader

CONTENTS

1 CAN YOU PLAY MACARTHUR PARK?

It was a cold, misty rain one night in late October. It was the kind of cold that can't be warmed. You can see your breath and feel it at the same time. The skin on your face tightens, you can't smile and it hurts to talk.

Joe Williams had his beige-on-brown taxicab parked outside Green's 24 hour Deli and Diner with his 'Out of Service' light on. Joe, like most people, a creature of habit, was sitting on his usual round, green bar stool, the one with the missing spring at the end of the counter nearest the window, so he could keep a watchful eye on his hack.

Joe usually got off duty at 2 a.m. It was only one-thirty. Joe had been having a terrible night. During nasty weather like that night people didn't venture out early, so there weren't a lot of people needing a ride home later. He had barely made enough in tips to pay for his cup of coffee.

"A buck a cup," Joe thought to himself, "and I drink my coffee black. That makes it doubly outrageous." Joe was just mumbling things to himself.

Mike, the night manager, had just poured Joe his free refill in the heavy bone-white porcelain cup he was drinking from. Steam was still pouring over the top of the cup as he held it just under his chin while he blew gently down on the surface in an effort to cool it off. The steam billowed up and fogged Joe's eye-glasses so completely that he couldn't see at all. With a grumt, he set his mug back down on the counter top and waited for his glasses to clear.

As his glasses went from an opaque to a spotty clear, Joe noticed a young woman clear at the other end of the counter smiling at him. At first he figured she was watching him make a fool of himself with his coffee cup. Being the good natured person that he was, Joe held up his cup to her in a toast, smiled, nodded to her, and began to sip on his much cooled-down Java.

What happened next took Joe completely by surprise. The young lady got up from her end of the counter, walked all the way to where Joe was sitting, and sat down near him. She was a 'looker' Joe noticed as she made her way toward him. She was wearing a blue print dress with an empire waistline and small lavender and white flowers on it. She was wearing a long overcoat too, but it wasn't buttoned and that's how he got a good look at what she was wearing. She had a kind face, not too much make-up, framed with jet black hair, just touching her shoulders. Her eyes were cobalt blue. She had a small sculptured, turned up nose with three freckles; her straight white teeth illuminated her perfect smile. She was a goddess, Joe thought.

Joe didn't say anything as she sat down next to him. He just sat and stared at her.

"Were you trying to get my attention?" she asked, feeling somewhat uncomfortable under his stare.

Joe was so taken back that he sat his coffee cup down too hard on the counter and he spilled it.

"Oh, Jesus, no. No, ma'am, I'm truly sorry if I caused you to come way down here thinkin' I was being fresh or anything." Joe stuttered to get the words out. He grabbed a handful of napkins from the silver and black dispenser on the counter and began to clean up his mess.

The pretty visitor didn't answer. She laughed a gentle laugh. It sounded like the jingling of silver bells to Joe, or the ringing of expensive crystal. When Joe spilled his coffee she jumped up at first thinking it might spill on her, then she sat back down, one stool away from Joe. As she did, her dress fell away from her knees, exposing her upper thigh and a large, nasty looking black and blue bruise.

"Oh my-oh my, look what you did to yourself," said Joe as he fumbled to compose himself while he continued to mop up his coffee spill with a handful of shredding, soaked, paper napkins. "Are you hurt, miss?"

Joe's face was turning red, he could feel himself embarrassing himself.

"I broke a heel and fell off the curb," the soft spoken voice replied. She opened her purse, extracted a blue shoe with a heel missing, and smiled a friendly smile.

Joe bent forward to get a closer look. In doing so he noticed she wasn't wearing shoes on either feet.

She noticed Joe's perplexed look. "Have you ever tried to walk with only one high heel?"

"Oh, my, no M'am," Joe managed to answer.

"I was running to catch the 42nd street bus, and got my heel caught in a heating grate. I fell, broke my heel, almost broke my leg, and I missed my bus. It was the last bus of the evening." She explained and she began to cry softly.

Joe, being the kind man that he was, was drawn in by her sad story. Her crying really upset Joe.

"Now, now, missy, please don't cry," Joe pleaded. He grabbed another handful of napkins and handed them to her so she could blow her nose and wipe her eyes.

"Mike, Mike, we need some more coffee down here, and bring a clean cup for the lady here." Joe bellowed.

"Thank you," she said with a sniffle.

"Careful now or you'll ruin your mascara," Joe said with a warm and reassuring smile.

Mike banged the coffee cup down on the counter. It was obvious Mike was having a bad night. "Do you want to run a tab?" He said sarcastically.

"Here, take my money," Joe said, "after all the business I bring you I should at least be entitled to a complimentary cup once in a while."

"Business, what business?" Mike snapped back as he walked along the counter towards the cash register to deposit the money. "You never eat anything, all you ever do is drink coffee and complain," he continued.

"Now that's just not true," Joe said as he started to

raise his voice. "Last Wednesday night I ate some lemon meringue pie, and it was stale I might add. But did I complain? No! I'm a gentleman, that's why."

"Pshaw!" was Mike's only retort as he waved a disgusted hand at Joe.

"Really," the raven-haired stranger pleaded, stress could be heard as she spoke, "please don't do this. I can't pay you back. I barely have bus fare; now that I've missed my bus I don't know what I'm going to do."

The genuineness of her entreaty touched the emotional side of Joe. In his typical blue-collar, abrupt fashion he tried to take charge.

"Look here, lady, my name is Joe." With that he proudly opened his wind-breaker and showed her his metro cab badge with his picture on it. "Please don't get so upset. Things aren't all that bad, really they aren't. I'm off duty and I'd be glad to drop you off; it's right on my way home anyway."

The woman, stifling a sniffle, broke out in a big smile. "Hi, Joe, my name is Jacquline, but all my friends call me Jackie." With that she held out her hand to shake Joe's, who took her forward move by surprise. "Thank you, Joe, that would help me out a lot. You're my knight in shining armor."

Joe felt himself blushing. "Shucks, miss."

"Jackie, Joe, call me Jackie. That is if you want to be my friend."

"Gosh, miss, I mean, Jackie, is a fella's name and you're much too beautiful to be called by a man's name."

"Thank you, Joe," said Jackie, returning the blush, "you really are a knight in shining armor." With that she got up and kissed Joe on his forehead.

5

Jackie moved to the stool closest to Joe, finished wiping the spill and joined Joe in his early morning cup of coffee. The two sat for more than a half an hour talking about nothing, and listening to the stories only lonely people tell, and sadder yet, only lonely people understand.

"Are you married, Joe?"

"I was, Jackie, for twenty years. Martha died of cancer three years ago." Joe continued to answer the question with the noticeable sound of regret in his voice, "We never had any kids, we just had each other," and his eyes filled with tears.

Then in an unexpected act of kindness, Jackie took a handful of napkins from the dispenser, and instead of handing them to Joe, patted his cheeks dry.

"It's getting late," said Joe as he got up; "Do you have anything I can carry? That's my cab parked just outside the front door."

"Just my purse, thanks."

Joe got up and waved good-bye to Mike. Mike was busy talking to one of the route delivery men who had come in for his breakfast and didn't notice Joe and Jackie leave. Green's was the only all night diner open on that end of town; consequently they get a lot of delivery men and late road crews coming in out of the weather.

As Joe held the door open for Jackie, the drizzle and the chill of the late night air slapped them gently in the face.

Joe ran over to his cab and held the back door open for Jackie. "Be careful not to slip and fall; once tonight is enough for anyone."

Jackie held her purse over her head and made a dash for the cab. "Thanks, Joe, you are a prince of a gentleman. I don't need to catch my death of cold on top of everything else that has happened, do I?"

Joe was holding the cab door open with one hand and held Jackie by the other so she could balance herself as she slipped in. Then Joe hurried around to the driver's side and slid behind the wheel. As he started the engine he asked, "Where to?"

"Thirty-ninth and Elm. I'm in the apartment building across the street from the corner dry-cleaners."

"I know exactly where it is. We should be there in twenty minutes or less."

Just like he always had, Joe let his cab warm up a few minutes before he turned his headlights on, then pulled away from the curb.

"You married, Jackie?"

"I was," came a soft spoken reply from the back seat. There was a brief pause, "I came home from work one night and all his things were gone. All the money in our joint account was too. We had one child that died from crib death before he was a month old. Harry, that was my husband, never ever got over it. He blamed me."

Friendly, talkative Joe was speechless. He wanted to say he was sorry, but that was senseless. Joe remembered when Martha died, people were always coming up to him and saying how sorry they were, like it was their fault. He didn't like that at all. He was upset with himself for not knowing how to handle the situation better.

Joe knew 39th and Elm because he'd been stiffed right around the corner from there just the week before. 39th and Elm wasn't a great place to live. They were all row homes. Not that row homes aren't nice, but these catered to a lot of section eight housing. Jackie seemed like a decent sort, but Joe couldn't see her living in an area that was better known for drugs and prostitution.

Joe knew better than to pre-judge people by where they lived. Once he took a fare into the ghetto. The fare was an elderly white man dressed better than most; nothing outstanding. He became a regular for a long time. For some reason the man and Joe hit it off. It was most likely because Joe was one of a very few cab drivers who would go into the ghetto, daylight only, of course.

Anyway, Joe didn't see the man for almost a year. Joe figured the man died or moved away. One day Joe got a book in the mail, Joe never orders books, so he was quite bewildered. On the back of the book was a picture of the old man. It turned out the man was a famous writer living in the ghetto doing research for his book. When Joe opened the book the author had signed the inside cover with a special note: "Joe, thanks for the help, I'll call you on my next trip to town."

Joe turned down 39th street, his wipers were on intermittent. Jackie leaned forward and tapped Joe on his shoulder.

"Three more blocks, I'm on the right side," Jackie said. "There is a big blue mail box right in front."

Joe slowed down. The alley was spotted with the occasional junk car. It was not a very nice neighborhood. Almost all of the ground level apartments had steel security bars over the windows, or they were boarded up.

Joe pulled his cab along the curb next to the graffiti painted mail box.

"I'll walk you to the door since it's this late at night," Joe said.

"No thanks, Joe," replied Jackie, "you've done enough already. I can manage from here. Thank you."

"I'll tell you what," Joe said as he turned and handed Jackie one of his business cards, "I'll sit here and watch you go inside then I'll leave." And almost as an afterthought he added, "And if I can be of future service, please call."

Jackie took Joe's business card, and to Joe's surprise kissed him on the back of his hand. Then she jumped, out slamming the door behind her, and skipped up the steps towards her apartment.

Joe watched Jackie enter the front of her building just like he told her he would. As he pulled away from the curb he noticed there wasn't the usual smattering of late night derelicts or passers by. The chilling drizzle probably had a lot to do with it.

He turned on his left turn signal as he approached the intersection and rounded the corner. Joe really didn't mind coming into neighborhoods like this. A lot of the cabbies Joe worked with refused to pick up or deliver passengers after dark for fear of being robbed. Joe figured ever since Martha died it didn't matter much what happened to him.

Joe was careful, he didn't take unnecessary chances. Besides, he carried a nickel plated colt 35 revolver under his front seat. He never even fired it; he always hoped if he had to it wouldn't be at another person.

Joe cracked his window to let the fresh smells of the night in and to help keep himself awake. He heard the sounds of sirens echoing off the walls of the row houses lining the streets like cement walls of a canyon.

Out of instinct Joe looked down at his speedometer just to make sure he wasn't going too fast; forty-seven in a forty mile per hour zone. The sounds were growing louder and the flashing blue lights were reflecting in his eyes off the rear-view mirror. He pulled over to the curb and let the police car pass with its lights and siren disturbing the night.

In the city sirens are almost commonplace. If it's not a police siren, it's a fire truck or an ambulance. In a town this size it seems as if there is always an emergency somewhere.

Joe continued along his way towards Church Street, a major north-south artery that would almost take him home. He heard the sounds of more and more sirens, as he was getting closer to them. Then just one block from Church Street he saw the bright lights of fire-trucks, police cars, and several ambulances, and the thick black smoke from a car on fire. The car was dangerously close to a gas station and the fire department was spraying foam on the car and the gas pumps.

A young policeman in a shiny rain coat was directing traffic around the accident scene by detouring them through a near-by parking lot. That forced Joe to go one block out of his way, past his turn.

Joe lived in a small two bedroom duplex in what was once an attractive middle-class neighborhood. It was still a decent place to live. The pavement was cracked, the curbs were crumbling, reflecting years of neglect and age. Most of the people living there were the same people Joe and Martha had come to know over the years. The mostly elderly residents were the original home owners. Young people weren't attracted to the neighborhood because the city had closed the local schools in order to consolidate and save money. Over the years the school buildings lay empty. Vandals had destroyed all the windows. Obscene graffiti covered the walls. It had become known as an area for crack/cocaine.

The residents formed a neighborhood watch, and said, enough is enough. They staged a sit-in at a city commissioner's meeting, voicing their disgust. The city finally gave in. They bull-dozed the school and turned the grounds into a neighborhood park with lots of flowers, lights, and playground equipment. They didn't fix the streets, but they managed to run off most of the drug dealers and that was important.

Joe pulled his cab into his driveway. He didn't have a garage. The city allowed parking on the street, except on Thursdays, because that's when the street cleaner came. As Joe was pulling into his driveway his headlights shone on the small bay window he had bought for Martha on their last Christmas together. Martha had always wanted one for her African violets. Joe couldn't see spending all that money just to have a place to put flowers. Finally, after years of nagging, Joe gave in and gave Martha her fancy window. She cried when they installed it. After Martha passed on all the plants died too; Joe wasn't much of a gardener.

Felix, Joe's black and brown house cat, was sitting in the Bay window where the violets used to grow. As always, as soon as Felix saw Joe's headlights he made a bee-line for the side door, jumped on the counter and greeted Joe as he came in. Felix always stood on the counter next to the door with his back arched and his tail held high, purring loudly for attention. Joe always scratched Felix between his ears and said "Hello, Felix, were you a good kitty today?"

Joe would usually pick Felix up, carry him to his easy-chair, and that's where Joe would fall asleep; in front of the TV, holding Felix.

Everyone in the neighborhood knew Joe and his taxi cab. Joe was always picking up groceries for someone, or taking the shut-ins to the doctor; never asking for, or collecting a penny. Every once-in-awhile Joe would get a nice pot roast, pie, or cake as a thank-you.

After Martha passed away it took Joe over a month just to figure out the buttons and dials on the washer and dryer. Still, after all this time, Joe occasionally forgot to take the clean clothes out of the washer, sometimes for days, before putting them in the dryer.

It was still raining the next morning when Joe woke up in his easy-chair with Felix asleep on his lap. It was later than usual; the soap operas had already come on TV. Martha used to watch soap operas all the time. In fact it was just about the only thing that Joe and Martha ever fought about. Martha had three soap operas that she followed like religion. Unless it was during a commercial, Martha wouldn't answer the phone or the door.

One Day Joe accidentally locked himself out of his cab so he called Martha to bring him his extra set of keys. Well, as luck would have it, Martha was watching her favorite soap and wouldn't answer the phone; even though Joe let it ring fifty times, or so he said.

Joe got so mad at Martha for not answering the

phone he finally called another cab to take him home to get his keys. They had a terrible fight; Martha and Joe were throwing ash trays and flower pots at one another. Someone, probably Joe, threw something that cracked the large picture window in the living-room. It was shortly after that Joe bought Martha the Bay Window. He also bought her an answering machine; one with a screening feature so she could hear the person leaving the message. At least that way if it was a real emergency she could answer the phone.

"Come on, Felix, it's time to eat."

Felix jumped down off Joe's lap with a loud thud.

"How can such a small cat make so much noise?" Joe asked Felix as if he were expecting a reply. Felix wasn't paying any attention. He was busy scurrying to the kitchen. Felix knew the routine. Each morning Joe would plug in the percolator, and while the coffee was brewing Joe would feed Felix and clean out his litter box. Joe cleaned Felix's litter box every morning except for Sunday; on Sunday Joe would change it completely.

After breakfast that usually consisted of three cups of coffee and a plain bagel Joe would clean his taxicab. Joe used to tell Martha, "Having a clean seat for the passenger to sit on was as important as wearing a clean shirt." Joe knew how important it was to leave the customer with a good impression.

Joe didn't always eat bagels for breakfast. In fact when Martha was alive she would feed him fresh blueberry hot-cakes and country ham. That was Joe's favorite; along with fresh biscuits and honey. Joe started having chest pains just before Martha passed. The doctor said it was because his cholesterol level

13

was too high. Joe would complain that the diet Martha put him on was more painful than his heart problems.

Joe liked taking care of Felix. He needed someone to care for, especially someone who returned the affection, even if it was only a cat.

Joe had a small shoe box where he kept lost and found items. Over the years the box was nearly filled with all sorts of things; eye glasses, loose change, unmatched earrings, beads from broken necklaces, pocket combs and such. Joe never kept anything he found. Once he found a wallet with over a hundred dollars in it. Joe called the man whose name and address was on the driver's license. The wallet had many credit cards, and the owner was amazed to find an honest person. The man offered Joe a reward, but Joe turned it down.

Joe told Felix he would be right back. Felix acted like he understood because he headed for the Bay window where he could watch. Joe tucked the little box under his arm and carried it out to his cab.

The first thing Joe saw when he opened the back door was a woman's high-heel shoe with a missing heel. Joe picked up the shoe and put it in the box. Then he lay half on the seat and reached under the seat and felt around until he found the missing heel and retrieved it.

Joe finished cleaning the floor mats and the ash trays. At one time Joe had a "Thank you for not smoking" sign in his cab but took it down. "After all," he reasoned, "these people are renting my cab, I can't tell them not to smoke, it's their money."

Joe finished cleaning his cab front and back. He looked up to see Felix sunning himself in the window.

Joe tapped on the glass, Felix pawed at Joe's finger in a friendly gesture.

Joe got dressed that morning and decided to go to town and buy a few things he needed for the house; kitty litter being one of them. Joe hated to shop. He never clipped coupons or read sale ads. He just went to the store and bought whatever he needed. One of Joe's chief gripes about shopping was having to stand in line. "Joe," his neighbors would say, "you can save a lot of money if you shop around."

Martha had been a good coupon clipper. Joe used to fuss at her because most of the bottles in the cupboard had missing labels. Martha had shoe boxes filled with coupons for just about anything you would ever want, even things like oil changes and tires for Joe. Martha had her own catalog system, she knew where everything was.

Joe went back to the kitchen and started to put the lost and found box back on the shelf. Before he did he took the broken shoe and heel out and placed them on the counter.

"I'll be back in a few hours," Joe hollered to Felix, "I've got some shopping to do."

Joe got in his cab, put on his seat belt and looked at himself in his rear-view mirror trying to decide whether or not he needed a hair cut. Joe's thinning, sandy colored hair did not show much signs of graying. He was a ruggedly handsome man in his mid-fifties.

Joe adjusted his mirrors and put on his cabby's cap. When Joe first began driving a hack, almost thirty years earlier, everyone wore a cap with an identifying badge on the bill. Fashions changed over the years and hats and uniforms were no longer in style. Joe didn't like that. Most of the cabbies driving now wore whatever they felt like, and it was all right with the company they worked for. Not Joe, he still wore a khaki shirt and trousers; and of course, a matching khaki hat.

Joe's first stop was the drug store down the street from his house where he bought cat litter and some personal things he needed. Then he drove across the parking lot to the dry-cleaners he used to keep his uniforms fresh. Martha had always taken much pride in making Joe look good. When Martha was alive she would never let Joe wear a shirt more than one day at a time before she washed and ironed it. Martha was proud of Joe.

"Good morning, Joe," said Oscar. Oscar was an Oriental guy who, together with his wife and family, ran the dry cleaning-shoe repair-alteration business, and had been for about a dozen years.

"Good morning, Oscar. How are the kids and your lovely wife?"

"Doing well. Thank-you for asking. Did you bring me something to clean today? In by nine, out by five."

"No, Oscar, I need a shoe repaired." Oscar's wife did the mending and Oscar repaired the shoes. Joe handed Oscar the broken shoe and heel. Oscar studied the broken pieces for a few seconds.

"I can fix this now while you wait. It's a clean break and will only take a few minutes."

"Gee, Oscar, that would be great. I will."

"Say, Joe," Oscar chided, "when did you start wearing ladies shoes?"

"Some lady left it in my cab last night, Oscar. She was down on her luck so I thought I'd fix it for her."

"You're a good man, Joe," said Oscar, "I'm glad to know you."

Joe just blushed.

Oscar went over to one of his machines and put the shoe in a vice-like device. He sanded a few rough spots and then super-glued the heel back in place. Then he put a small screw in the back for extra support. Oscar blew on the heel for a brief second and when he was comfortable that the glue was sufficiently dry, he polished it.

It was easy to see Oscar took pride in his work.

"Here you are, Joe, all done, just like new."

"Thanks, Oscar, how much do I owe you?"

"You're a good Samaritan, Joe, I'll help too. This one's on the house."

"Thanks, Oscar, I really mean that."

"Don't mention it, Joe."

W.J. "Duke" Mader

2 CLOSING THE FAMILY ALBUM

Jackie Jones, the not-so-young divorcee Joe had given a ride to, lived in a three story walk-up in what was once a nice part of town. Twenty years earlier there had been an auto parts manufacturing plant near by and the many local residents who worked there could take the bus to work from home. It wasn't long after the plant closed that the people began to gradually move away. A lot of the renters moved out as soon as their leases were up. Most homeowners stayed only until their houses sold.

Landlords had a hard time keeping the units filled because there wasn't much to attract new tenants to the area, except for lower rent. As the rents went lower so did the caliber of the renters. Slowly, over the years more and more buildings were getting boarded up. That gave the graffiti artists new canvases to paint.

As the neighborhood began to decay the quality of

life did, too. Prostitution and drug dealing became more of a way of life rather than the exception. By now almost all of the original inhabitants from the "good old days" had either moved away or died.

Jackie lived on the second floor, just high enough above the street not to have to worry about having bars on her windows. She had a bedroom, living-dining room combination, a small kitchen with a gas stove, and a bath with a tub--no shower. It could be said that Jackie lived in the fringe area. That is to say her building had all its windows, and almost no graffiti. But the fringe was getting frayed, decaying slowly like a cancer eating its host.

Jackie had only lived there for a few months. The main reason she moved in was because the landlord advertised two months free rent for tenants signing a year's lease. It was a common way of enticing people to move in.

It was a drastic change from the upper middle-class section of town known as Dunkirk where Jackie and Harry had lived. Dunkirk had all single family homes thick with flowers and trees. Jackie's then husband, Harry, was an accountant for a law firm. Harry was Jackie's high-school sweetheart. In fact Jackie and Harry were virgins when they got married. Their strict religious up-bringing helped them stay away from drugs and sex before marriage. He had a good job, and he had worked his way to the top in just a few short years. Harry's job was filled with stress trying to keep things balanced. After Harry Jr. died of SIDS, Harry went off the deep end. Not only did he move out, but he quit his job, cleaned out most of the house and joint bank account, and left town.

Jackie's job as a receptionist at a dental clinic

didn't pay her nearly enough to make the mortgage payment on her expensive home. She put the house on the market hoping to just break even. But the bank foreclosed before she could sell it . She had never so much as balanced a check book or paid a bill and was having trouble just dealing with reality.

Jackie made a good receptionist. Her eyes had a natural sparkle and her easy smile relaxed everyone who came to her desk to register for their appointment allaying the fears of drills and long needles most patients brought in with them. Jackie's girl-next-door appearance and mannerisms helped her to relate to people of all ages and walks of life.

Her naiveté, while charming, worked against her as she would often find herself too trusting and not favoring the security of caution. Jackie could never bring herself to be skeptical. It was the way she was brought up. Her father used to say, "Your word is your bond," Jackie thought other people were the same way.

Now that Jackie was single for the first time since she was a freshman in high school, she found herself facing a range of emotions she had never known before. Jackie had gone from the security of living at home to being married. She never had to worry about a place to live, food to eat, or companionship.

Harry, her high-school sweetheart, was always the book-worm type; very religious and considered by many as the class nerd. Harry had no outside interests, just school.

When Harry and Jackie first got married they agreed to practice birth control. They wanted to wait and do things right, so-to-speak. They wanted to save before they had children. They wanted to wait until

Harry made enough money so Jackie could quit her job and devote her life to the family as Harry's mother had done.

Harry decided it should be his traditional role to be the provider. That role appealed to Harry, who had never known how to command respect. That would guarantee his dominance over a wife and family. Since Jackie and Harry had both been raised in that type of atmosphere, it only seemed logical.

Harry and Jackie were married for almost ten years before Harry got promoted to senior accountant and got a huge raise in pay. With the promotion Harry became a changed man. Their sexual activity went from seldom or rarely to frequently and often. Those love making sessions, even though performed mainly for the act of procreation, awakened a side of Jackie that had been dormant all her life. Harry had never been a sensual man and Jackie ignored those private feelings she experienced as the devil's work.

Now that Harry was intent on creating a family, his sexual ritual, although basic and without much creativity, was becoming somewhat varied just because of the frequency. In the very beginning Harry was quick to climax leaving Jackie to wonder "what happened?" Weeks later it was taking longer for Harry to ejaculate. Somehow that related to more pleasure for Jackie. Jackie soon learned how to control Harry's enthusiasm, so she could prolong her own enjoyment; Harry never caught on.

The whole experience began to unravel when Jackie went to the Doctor for her monthly visit and surprised Harry with the good news; she was pregnant. Harry cut her off sexually. His excuse was that he didn't want to do anything to hurt the baby.

Jackie was crushed; her body was tuned to anticipating their almost daily sexual ritual. Her needs had blossomed beyond her control.

At the same time Harry found out Jackie was pregnant he had her quit work and stay home. Jackie used the time to read books on 'Motherhood' and 'Parenting.' Jackie began to read 'Romance' books to help satisfy the inner itch that had developed. Reading lead to regular forms of masturbation since Harry had put her body "off limits."

When Jackie was far enough along to have her first sonogram and found out the child she was carrying was a boy, Harry went ballistic with enthusiasm. It was undoubtedly the happiest day of his life. He told everyone he knew or met that Harry Jr. was on his way. Harry actually became involved with helping Jackie decorate the baby's room, traditional blue of course. He picked out expensive furniture and more stuffed animals than there was room to put them in. Harry bought special cigars with "It's a boy" printed on them months before the baby was born.

Harry was a good provider, even though his physical attraction to Jackie had quickly faded. Jackie missed the sexual encounters, brief as they were. She filled her days cooking, cleaning, reading about babies and trying to suppress an increasing need for self-fulfillment.

In the beginning Jackie was ashamed of her need to fondle herself; however in one of the books she read there was a reference to some husbands abandoning their wives physically during their time of gestation. Jackie decided this was the natural course that came with carrying a child and eventually brushed those guilt feelings aside, and allowed her need for fulfillment to be stronger than her feelings of guilt.

Jackie gradually purchased creams and mechanical devices to aid her in self-fulfillment. Her hunger for physical fulfillment was becoming increasingly apparent. On several occasions she woke Harry up in the middle of the night by caressing him.

"What the hell do you think you're doing?" demanded a mostly asleep Harry.

"What does it feel like I'm doing, dear," said the soft spoken Jackie.

"Well, can't you see I'm trying to get some sleep? I work, remember. I don't stay home all day and watch TV."

"But, Harry...."

"Don't but Harry me. What has gotten into you woman, are you nuts? You know we've discussed this before. Topic closed."

She thought that if she got him aroused he would respond by completing the sexual act. Instead the only thing that got aroused was Harry's temper. On those occasions he would get up and sleep on the couch.

It was nights like those and memories of others that caused Jackie to cry herself to sleep. Jackie was in full bloom as a woman; with child she was full circle. She knew new energies and sensations from her sexual side. She carried a glow and a new level of self-confidence that even her husband recognized.

The baby was full term and born on a Saturday morning. That made Harry happy--he didn't have to miss work. The first week Jackie was home from the hospital, Harry arranged for a private duty nurse. That was Harry's way of sharing in the responsibility.

The night before Harry Jr. was to be baptized, he died of crib death. The death of a child is so tragic that no spoken or written word can define the event. Everything in the house died that night.

After her baby was buried Jackie went back to work as a receptionist for the same dentist she had worked for before. The pay wasn't much but it was all Jackie knew how to do, and it helped to take her mind off the tragedy. The death of her son was followed by the disappearance of her husband the same month.

Jackie's first thoughts were of suicide. Her preacher along with close friends helped her through her toughest times. Jackie found the inner strength needed and decided to pull her life together to find out just where she stood before things really got out of hand.

It didn't take long before Jackie realized she had far too many bills to pay with the meager wages she took home. That meant she would have to sell her home and find a place she could afford which wouldn't be much. The very thought of giving up her dream home greatly depressed her, however she also knew that she needed to distance herself from the memories of the loss of a child and a failed marriage.

Too proud to go back to her parents because of their strong religious beliefs against divorce, Jackie sold most of her belongings and moved to her current address. It was on a major bus route and the ad read "first two months rent free." After moving in her few remaining belongings, and extensive wardrobe, Jackie spent much of the first two months crying. She tried to hide her pain, but could not. Those who knew her best thought it was the burden of losing a child that caused her distress. It was not. Rather, it was the personal disgrace Jackie felt every time her bus stopped in front of her walk-up. She would hesitate to see the condition of the neighborhood and realized the personal loss of her pride and dignity. Jackie always knew Harry hadn't been a model husband, but he had been a good provider, and she gave him high marks for that.

The night Joe, the cab driver, had given her a ride home was a repeat performance of the kind of days Jackie was growing weary of. Her only child had died and she carried the guilt. Her marriage ended in divorce, and she carried the guilt. She couldn't afford to support herself the way Harry did and she carried the guilt. Her self esteem was at an all time low, and she didn't care. Jackie was once a lady whose lips never touched alcohol or tobacco. Now she looked favorably to going to fashionable lounges looking seductive so men would buy her liquor. She wasn't good at smoking. She still didn't know what to do with her hands. She would only smoke when offered, but she was practicing.

* * * * *

Every journey starts with the first step. It was no different for Jackie. One day at work Dr. Jefferies, the dentist Jackie worked for, asked her to go to town and pick up a gold crown from the lab that did their work. Dr. Jefferies needed the crown for an eight-thirty am appointment and the lab said they were short handed and couldn't deliver it until noon. Dr. Jefferies told the lab he would have someone pick it up for him.

"Jackie, I need you to do me a special favor," Dr. Jefferies stated as he approached his receptionist's desk. Dr. Jefferies was a portly, late sixtyish, balding, grand, fatherly figure who took extra time to be patient with Jackie. In all the time Jackie had worked for Dr. Jefferies, he had never made an improper advance towards her or spoken words that might offend her tender nature.

"Yes, Doctor, what can I do for you?" Jackie replied with her usual enthusiasm.

3 FIVE-STAR EXPERIENCE

Jackie walked on a thickly carpeted floor into the main lobby of the five star hotel remembering the thrill of her first visit. In front of her was a golden horseshoe shaped stairway surrounded with an ornately carved, gold colored hand-rail, and steps thick with plush red carpeting. Overhead was the largest, most beautiful crystal chandelier she had ever seen. It reminded her of the one she saw in the movie "Gone with the Wind." The rush of luxury made Jackie feel like a movie star.

The long hall to the left of the registration desk led to the lounge. Jackie's heart was pounding under her dress. She nodded and smiled to several of the attendants she passed.

The door to the lounge was two steps above the lounge floor. Jackie hesitated on the top step; she had an unobstructed view of the long bar on the right, the dance floor in front of the stage in the center, and the many small tables with winged back chairs to the left near the piano player. The buffet was set up on the edge of the dance floor; Jackie was hungry, she hadn't eaten all day, but decided she should order a drink first. She felt it would be improper of her to sit at the bar so she made her way towards the tuxedo clad piano player and sat at a small round table with two chairs.

A young man wearing a white jacket, black trousers, and a black bow tie put a napkin down in front of her.

"May I get you something from the bar?"

Jackie's voice locked. She looked at him and couldn't speak. That made her embarrassed enough to want to walk out. Jackie swallowed hard and nodded yes.

"Perhaps the lady would care for a glass of wine."

Jackie was having an anxiety attack. She couldn't breathe, and nodded yes once again.

"May I suggest a Zinfandel," said the server without staring.

Again Jackie nodded in the affirmative and the waiter left. Jackie sat back against her high-backed chair and closed her eyes for just a second to compose herself. She remembered how excited she had been coming here on her first visit. The orchestra was playing and the room filled with elegant people. She was happy then, and she missed it now.

"Excuse me miss, are you waiting for someone?"

The sound was close by. Jackie opened her eyes to see a tall man dressed in a camel colored suit, a frilly white shirt with a leather beaded string tie and boots standing in front of her. She jumped slightly in her chair at the start.

"I'm sorry if I startled you, ma'am. But I couldn't help but to notice you sitting here all by yourself; I'm in town for a convention and was hoping I could sit with you."

"I, er, that is to say...," Jackie was dumbstruck and found it hard to compose a sensible sentence.

The tall, gray-haired man sat down on the chair opposite her and placed his cocktail glass on the small round table between them. Just then the waiter brought Jackie her glass of wine.

"Put that on my bill," the man told the waiter who nodded that he understood.

"Oh, please, no. Don't do that." Jackie finally got some words out.

"Ma'am, my name is Phil, I'm from Fort Worth Texas. Please excuse my lack of manners, I should have introduced myself right off."

"I'm glad to meet you, I'm sure, but really, Mr. Phil, I can buy my own drink."

"No, pretty lady, Phil is my first name, and I'm sure you can buy your own drink, but I'm on an expense account, and if you won't tell, neither will I." Without taking a breath Phil continued, "Have you tried out the fabulous buffet?"

"No, I haven't. I was just going to when you sat down," Jackie replied, beginning to get her composure back.

"May I escort you to the food table? It would be my honor."

Jackie was hungry, and didn't really want to walk across the floor by herself. Hunger was winning the battle with discretion. "I suppose it would be all right," she said, fighting the impulse to show emotion.

Phil held out his hand to her. The mark of

chivalry impressed Jackie and for the first time since his arrival, she smiled.

"I don't mind calling you 'pretty lady' unless you have some other name you'd like to be called."

Jackie stood up in front of her escort and said, "Jackie, my name is Jackie."

Jackie turned to place her purse on the chair, then, remembering the merchandise she was entrusted with, tucked her purse under her arm and left with Phil for the buffet table.

At one end of the long table were the cold hors d'oeuvres arranged in a floral composition. In the middle of the table were a variety of small dishes filled with sauces and dips, followed by the shiny stainless covered trays, heated with small cans of sterno, that contained chicken wings, small Italian sausages, and some kind of tri-colored pasta.

Jackie took a plate with several napkins, and although her original intent was to load up with fresh vegetables, she piled her plate high with the meats she wouldn't allow herself to buy. She looked at her plate and was embarrassed until she looked across the table at Phil who himself had built a small fortress with food. That made her smile and encouraged her self confidence.

"I hope you're about ready," Phil said to Jackie, "because I'm plum running out of room."

"Well," answered Jackie with a new found strength in her voice, "we can always move our chairs closer to the buffet table."

Phil just laughed, a strong, masculine laugh. Not at all like Harry's laugh that tended to be high pitched and more of a giggle than a laugh. Jackie liked the way Phil laughed.

"So, tell me, Jackie, what brings you to this fine hotel tonight-- surely not the buffet?"

Jackie felt a bit flushed. It was indeed the offer of free food that initially caught her attention.

"I was in the neighborhood on business and thought I would drop in for a visit."

"Have you ever been here before?" questioned Phil.

"Just once, about three years ago with my husband. It was a political thing."

"Oh, then you're married?" asked Phil sitting up straight as if he were looking for a way out.

Jackie took a drink of wine, and a chicken wing before answering. "My husband ran off and left me after our son died."

There was a moment of silence while Phil measured his words before replying.

"I'm sorry to hear that," said Phil relaxing somewhat, "about both losses."

"Losing my son was truly a tragedy," said Jackie with a fading voice, "losing my husband wasn't."

"Was he abusive?" asked Phil digging for information while changing the subject of the infant's death.

"Not in the usual manner." Jackie hesitated and said, "He was a good provider." For some reason she felt the need to defend the man who had run away and left her in a financial nightmare.

"I assume he left you with the house and a substantial settlement." Phil continued to probe.

Jackie didn't want to talk anymore, she finished her wine and placed the glass down on the marble table between them. "I really must be going."

"Please, if I offended you I apologize. Please let

me buy you one for the road, of course I mean that figuratively. And we have yet to try the pastries they have just added to the buffet."

Again Phil stood up before Jackie and offered her his hand. The attention was as welcomed as the food. Jackie had denied herself contact with anyone who didn't work with her. She smiled and placed her hand in his. Jackie enjoyed being treated like a lady.

The two spent several minutes looking for strawberry filled tarts; Jackie said those were her favorite. When they got back to their table, a filled glass of wine awaited. This glass went down easier and faster than the first.

The piano player began to delight the ears of those in attendance. Jackie once again closed her eyes and leaned back in her chair just to listen.

Phil was intoxicated with Jackie's natural beauty and naive manners. He leaned back in his chair and drank in Jackie's charms.

"Do you have a favorite song?" Phil finally said breaking the silence.

"Oh, my yes," Jackie said without hesitating. "It's an old song, one from my youth. Harry, that was my husband, thought it was stupid, so I haven't heard it for a very long time."

That was just the answer Phil was hoping for. He summoned the waiter to their table.

"So, tell me Jackie, what is this favorite song of yours?"

"He'll not know it," giggled Jackie, the effects of the wine beginning to show: "Mac Arthur Park."

Phil wrote the song title on a napkin, folded a ten dollar bill in it and handed the napkin to the waiter with orders to give it to the piano player.

"I don't believe I remember the song." Phil addressed Jackie.

The waiter returned with another glass of wine.

"It's a silly song. At least Harry said so. The words don't make a whole lot of sense, but the music is really pretty. When I was very young I would play the song over and over on my record player." As Jackie spoke her voice and memories drifted back to a more pleasant time. Jackie finished eating her tart and without realizing what she was doing, drank the whole glass of wine down in one tilt.

Jackie leaned back in her chair once again, relaxed and feeling talkative. The alcohol was beginning to loosen the bonds of inhibition.

"Now it's your turn to talk, Phil. What do you do back in Texas? Do you know J.R. Ewing?"

Phil laughed and Jackie listened to his mellow masculine laugh, very much enjoying the sound.

"My family owns a feed mill. There is a lot of corn and oats grown in Texas, and the farmers need a place to mill them. And you're not the first person to ask me if I knew J.R." Phil answered her question straight away with a big smile that further gave Jackie cause to relax.

Then, just as if it had been scripted, the piano player began the harmonious sounds of Mac Arthur Park. The sounds filled Jackie's head and she squealed with approval.

Phil sat back and watched.

Another glass of wine arrived.

"I really must go," said Jackie at the end of her song. "I have to get up early and deliver a package to the dentist I work for."

"You work for a dentist?" Phil sat up and leaned

towards Jackie.

"Yes, I have to support myself somehow. It's the only thing I know how to do," Jackie responded somewhat light-headed.

Phil wasn't prepared for the answer. For some reason he pictured Jackie as being a financially liberated woman.

In a fatherly way Phil continued, "A dental office surely can't pay a lot."

Jackie's voice became almost a whisper; her eyes welled with tears.

"To tell you the truth, Phil, it's been all I can do just to break even each month. I never wrote a check until after my husband left. I've never been so alone and scared in my whole life."

"What about your family? Can't they help you?"

"My parents don't believe in divorce; they've abandoned me." Jackie sniffed, then continued, "Imagine, parents abandoning a thirty-five year old child." Jackie put the handkerchief Phil had handed her to her cheeks to pat away the tears.

Phil was at a loss for words. His experience guided his judgment.

The piano player continued to play.

Phil stood up and extended his hand.

Jackie accepted not knowing why. "Do you want to go back to the buffet table again?" she questioned.

Phil did not answer. Instead he took her to the middle of the dance floor and began to waltz. Jackie was too taken back to say anything. She put her arm on his waist and danced for the first time in years. Jackie loved to dance. Harry didn't have time.

Phil had a strong physique, deliberate moves and a cologne that Jackie found more intoxicating than the wine. Phil and Jackie danced each dance until the piano player took a break. By then Jackie had her head firmly on Phil's chest, and was holding him tight. As her body pressed his she felt him stir beneath his belt. She pressed harder. The wine was well mixed in Jackie's veins. Not being a drinker she was not in full possession of her faculties.

Phil walked Jackie back to their table. Jackie sat there silent and motionless for several moments. Tears again filled her eyes as she remembered her fall from better times.

"I must go," she said, "I can't afford to get fired, I really do need this job."

"Okay," said Phil in a soft, reassuring manner, "but come on up to my room so you can wash your face and straighten out your make-up before you leave, and while your attending to that I'll have the door-man call a cab."

Jackie had no sense of mistrust, so she nodded her head in agreement.

4   THE FIRST ENCOUNTER

As Jackie got up to leave with Phil she lost her balance and had to reach for the table to steady herself. That in turn tipped the table just enough to allow their near empty drinking glasses to fall to the carpeted floor.

"No harm done," said Phil as he reached down to pick them up.

"I'm terribly sorry, I'm not usually clumsy," said Jackie as she began to cry. She knew she had embarrassed herself and was feeling awkward with the inclusion of too much alcohol.

"Look," said Phil holding the glasses up with a warm and reassuring smile, "no harm done, they didn't break."

Jackie took a firm grip of Phil's arm; not wanting to loose her balance again and make a fool of herself. She tucked her purse under her arm and the two left towards the main reception area of the hotel to where the elevators were located.

The bright lights of the foyer glared after the dark

and soft lights of the lounge. Jackie stopped just before the elevator.

"Phil, I want to thank you for your kindness. However, I feel it would be unwise of me to follow you to your room. Would you please just call me a taxi."

"Pretty lady," Phil responded with a low, soft voice, "if you'll look down at your dress, you'll see that when you got up you spilled some wine on your lap. If you don't come up and wash it out it will stain, I'm sure."

Jackie looked down at her dress. Sure enough there was a spot about the size of a small envelope on her upper thigh.

"Well, okay, but just for a moment."

The elevator door opened, and a young man and lady got off. Jackie and Phil got on and pressed seven. "I'm in room seven sixty-one," Phil proclaimed.

Jackie didn't answer, she was dizzy from all the wine and dancing. The elevator stopped at the seventh floor. Phil waited for Jackie to get out first, then led her down the hall to his room. The key to the door was like a credit card only it had small holes in it. Phil inserted the card into the slot and a green light appeared over the key hole. Phil turned the knob and held the door open for Jackie.

Jackie took a few steps into the room and stood motionless.

"My heavens," she said in astonishment, "your room is bigger than my apartment." Phil was staying in one of the hotel's finer luxury suites. It had two bedrooms, a small kitchen-breakfast nook, and a great room with a fireplace. Jackie literally walked around with her mouth open looking at the beautiful original oil paintings and statuary.

Phil smiled. "The bathroom is over there, and there is a large terry-cloth bathrobe hanging behind the door. Put it on while you're cleaning your dress."

The bathroom was bigger than Jackie's living room. It had a hot tub and a shower in it. There were wall to wall mirrors and a small crystal chandelier hanging in the middle. It even had a bidet. Jackie knew what that was from reading about them in health class, although she had never seen one. The carpet was a thick burnt-orange sculptured shag. The faucets were golden. Jackie's head was spinning in luxury. She took the bathrobe off the hook and shut the door.

She removed her shoes and placed them by the hot tub. The next thing she took off was her dress. She stood briefly and looked at herself in the full length mirror behind the door. She stood erect, sucked her small tummy in and stood sideways admiring her still firm body. She put the oversized robe on and had to turn up the sleeves several turns so as not to get them wet. Carefully, Jackie turned on the cold water and folded her dress so only the spot with the wine could be washed. She scrubbed the fabric back and forth several times. When she was satisfied the stain wouldn't set she rung the dress out as best she could.

Jackie carried her partly wet dress back out to the living area where the fire place was.

"Phil, do you mind if I lay my dress over a chair by the fire place for just a few minutes so it will dry faster?"

"Of course not. Here, let me help." With that

Phil took the dress from Jackie and draped it over a chair near the fire place.

"Please, sit down. I have something I would like to show you. I think it will make you happy," Phil said as he led Jackie to the sofa, with thick goose-down filled pillows. Then he placed a crystal glass filled with wine down on the hand carved cherry-wood coffee table in front of her.

Phil walked over to a panel filled with switches. He turned the first one and the fire in the fire place came on. The second one turned the lights down and the third one turned on the music.

"While you were cleaning up I called one of the local radio stations that plays "oldies" music. In just two minutes a special request will play, Phil said with a gleam in his eye.

Phil had taken off his jacket and was still wearing the long sleeve white dress shirt with the cuffs rolled up. Jackie sat in amazement saying nothing.

Then after the mandatory "word from our sponsor" the radio station began to play "Mac Arthur Park." Phil turned the volume up.

"May I have this dance?" he asked as he held out his hand. Jackie was drunk with the enchantment of the moment. She once again placed her hand in his and the two began to slow dance across the carpeted floor.

Phil held Jackie tightly to him. Jackie's head was swimming. Never had Harry shown such attention. She pressed herself closer to Phil and felt him become aroused. She hesitated. Phil looked down at her with his kindly smile, and Jackie on her tip-toes, reached up and gently kissed him.

The music played on, but the dancing stopped.

Phil kissed her back as gently as he had been all evening. It was Jackie's tongue that found it's way into Phil's mouth first. Jackie placed both hands on Phil's face and kissed him hard.

Phil reached down and untied Jackie's robe, and she let it fall to the ground while she worked to free his belt. It only took seconds for the two to find themselves back on the sofa. Phil had his head buried between Jackie's naked breasts. Jackie was pulling at his hair directing him on top of her. She was wet with anticipation. She climaxed almost as soon as he entered her.

For the next two hours their naked bodies touched one another in ways not shown in movie houses. Jackie kept climaxing, one after another. She had saved up for so long she couldn't control the release of emotions.

Finally Jackie collapsed on top of Phil and went to sleep. It was almost dawn when Jackie awakened to see the pinks and oranges of morning begin to creep over the horizon.

She looked down at the still sleeping Phil and was horrified. What had she done? What must he think of her? Quietly she slipped off her host, picked her now dry dress off the chair and returned to the bathroom with her under clothing to get dressed. Jackie looked at her watch; it was almost six in the morning. She knew she wouldn't have time to go back home and change and still get to work on time. That meant she would have to wear the same outfit to work two days in a row; something she had never done in her life before.

She looked down at the bidet, and although she wanted desperately to use it, she knew she didn't have the time. With one last look in the mirror, a tuck here and there, she was satisfied she looked presentable.

When she opened the bathroom door to sneak out, there stood Phil, wearing the terry-cloth bath robe.

"I didn't mean to keep you so late," he said apologetically.

"You didn't," replied Jackie in a softly embarrassed voice.

"I've called a taxi. They said there would be one here in ten minutes."

"Thank you, Phil." Jackie turned to face him, then turned away, looking for the right words. "I'm sorry if I've given you the wrong impression about me. I mean about last night...."

"Please don't say anything to ruin last night," Phil interrupted, "it was beautiful. Thank you."

Jackie was embarrassed, she looked at Phil, but not in the eye. She just couldn't make herself.

Phil walked over to her with her purse in his hand. "I'm going back to Texas today, and I will never enjoy someone's company as much as I enjoyed yours last night."

With that Phil handed Jackie her purse and twenty dollars.

"Here, this is for your cab fare."

"Oh, no!" said Jackie in a firm voice, "I can't take money, that would be sinful."

"Remember," said Phil in a softly reassuring voice, "I'm on an expense account, you're not. Please take the money for the cab. It would make me feel more comfortable knowing you'll be all right."

Phil hesitated as if to kiss her. Jackie took her purse and the twenty dollars. "Thank you, Phil, for being such a gentleman. I had forgotten there were such people still left on earth." Jackie turned and left.

Jackie allowed the doorman to open the cab door for her. As she left the Biltmore she looked over her shoulder for one last memory. She had the cab take her directly to work. When she arrived it was only a few minutes past seven. The office didn't open till eight. Jackie had a key, and a plan to save face.

"Wait here," she told the cab driver, "I'll be right back." With that Jackie opened the door to the office and went in. She took the package from the dental lab out of her purse and placed it on Dr. Jefferies desk with a note; "I'm running a fever and don't think I can make it in today, here is your package. PS. I'll call you after lunch. Jackie."

Jackie returned to her waiting cab and gave him directions to her apartment. Jackie was dreading going home, after spending a night in what some would call the lap of luxury.

5   SECOND CHANCE TAKEN

The cab pulled up in front of Jackie's apartment about seven forty-five that morning. The fare was fourteen-fifty; she handed the cabby a twenty and told him to keep it. Jackie stood quietly on the sidewalk in front of her apartment and took a hard look at where she lived. It was a depressing sight. The people who lived there were nice enough, but they would never pass for what some people would call "society."

Actually, Jackie never considered herself a socialite. But she knew the opportunity was there if she had wanted to press the situation. Some of the wives Harry's partners had were regular attendees of social functions; Jackie had the same opportunities, but turned them down. She was a home-body.

Jackie stood motionless with the train of thoughts roaring through her mind, unaware of the morning traffic behind her on the streets or the passers-by on the sidewalk. A shudder of reality brought her back.

At first she thought she would cry, in desperation and regret. She did not.

Jackie made her way up the steps to her apartment. There was a new "For Rent" sign on the front door of the lobby with a phone number to call. There were only four apartment to each floor, two facing the street and two facing the alley. Jackie's apartment faced the alley. At first the thought of facing the alley upset Jackie, until she learned how much quieter the alley side was. She was glad it was the only one available at the time she signed her lease.

Jackie went in and locked the door behind her; she had a dead bolt and a chain lock. Jackie was scared to death of being beaten or robbed. Every night she would go to sleep with the radio on in the living room so if someone was thinking of breaking in they would hear sounds and go somewhere else.

Jackie placed her purse on the kitchen table, which was also the dining room table, and opened the refrigerator door to pour herself a glass of instant orange juice. Jackie always made the juice at half strength; that way it would last longer. She set the glass on the table and placed the juice jar back in the fridge.

When Jackie sat down to take a drink she remembered spilling the glass of wine and wondered if the stain on her dress was gone. She hadn't bothered to check yet. Jackie got up and stepped out of her dress and held it close to the small kitchen window. No stain. She smiled, folded the dress and placed it over the back of a chair. As she sat quietly drinking her watered down orange juice she remembered she still had the receipt for the gold crown in her purse. She opened her purse to retrieve the receipt so she wouldn't forget to take it to work the next day.

Jackie stood up quickly, as if she had just sat on a needle, and in doing so knocked her chair over. There in the bottom of her purse was a wad of money. She grabbed it, unrolled five one hundred dollar bills and a note written on a cocktail napkin. The note read, "Don't forget to pay your rent. Remember I'm on an expense account-Phil"

Jackie stood shaking as if she had just come from a cold swim. "No, no, this isn't right," she shouted out loud. She ran to the phone in the bedroom, tears streaming down her face, and called the Biltmore.

"Hello, desk. I need to speak with Phil in room seven sixty one. No, I don't know his last name, what difference does it make. I want to talk to the person in room seven sixty one."

There was a brief pause, "What do you mean he's already checked out? No thank you, no message." Jackie hung up the phone and sat in a sculptured pose for minutes. Then she spread the five one hundred dollar bills on her bedspread and re-read the note. Phil must have felt sorry for her and this was his way of helping out.

This was Jackie's last free month of rent. She had been worried where the money would come from, and this was like a gift from heaven, she thought. Still, the whispers from her soul were telling her she had sold her body and that those carnal sins would cast her into eternal damnation. Jackie lay across her bed and cried for hours. Had she succumbed to the sins of desire, was she a harlot, or did she merely experience an act of human kindness. After all, she didn't ask for money, and Phil had never offered any.

Jackie was sure if he had she would have surely left before the evening went as far as it did.

For almost an hour, Jackie lay on her back looking at the ceiling. Her life was a mess, she needed a better paying job, she wasn't trained to do anything else, and she needed rent money. Those things were absolutes.

"Well, I guess I could always get married again," Jackie said out loud, "but first I would need to meet a man who would have me." Then she began to cry once more. It was a soft desperate cry. The kind that starts deep down in your soul and makes your body tremble as the shudder of desperation wells its way to the surface and tears slide effortlessly down the cheeks.

Sitting up in bed and looking at the money spread out before her she continued to hold a one sided conversation, in an effort to distract herself from her pain.

"I could sell drugs...," she shouted out loud. "No, I don't know a drug from an aspirin, so that's out." Then flashing back on the previous night's escapade, "I could pick out a good corner and sell myself," she said in a self- castigating tone. Her eyes welled up with tears, but she wouldn't let herself cry. Her one-night stand with Phil was perfectly honest, so some would say, nothing more than a chain of events with a happy ending. Jackie knew her personal frustrations had been building long before Harry had left her.

Jackie went to her small bathroom and started running a tub filled with hot water. She added her favorite bubble bath and skin conditioner. Jackie finished undressing and put her soiled clothing in the hamper. She looked down at the stained toilet with a cracked lid and remembered the gold, ornate bidet. Her personal hygiene was not going to have to suffer, she told herself. She could just close her eyes and pretend.

By the time Jackie had finished cleaning herself on the inside it was time to soak the outside. The tub was filled with hot water and foamy bubbles. She slid into the steamy bath up to her neck. The bubbles tickled her nose.

With her eyes closed she relived the sensual moments she had with Phil the evening before. She remembered the strength of his touch, and the gentleness. She touched herself in the same way he did, trying to stimulate excitement, trying to find the same spot to render herself numb with fulfillment.

Those thoughts brought Jackie the stimulation she needed to complete the act by herself. "Of course," she rationalized, "I can't reproduce his smell or the feeling of his coming inside me, but this is the next best thing."

The phone rang. Jackie was forced back to reality.

"Hello, Jackie, how are you feeling?"

"Good afternoon, Dr. Jeffries," said Jackie recognizing the voice and checking her watch, "I'm much better, thanks for asking."

"Is there anything you need, or that we can get for you?"

"No, sir, I just need some rest. Tomorrow is Saturday, so by Monday I should be good as new."

"You're a good woman Jackie, we need you to be healthy. It doesn't look good for our receptionist to have the sniffles." Dr. Jefferies said good-bye and hung up. Jackie sat listening to the hum of the disconnected line as if she were waiting for it to reconnect. Then, as if in a hypnotic daze, hung the receiver up, placed her face in her hands and began to cry once again. Jackie had lied to Dr. Jefferies. She had never done that before. Jackie was wondering what terrible kind of transformation she was going through; drinking, lying and spending the night with a strange man.

After Jackie had cried herself out, she fell asleep, still naked from her bath, and with matted hair that dried itself. When she awoke it was as if she had a revelation. The money was a gift, it was hers, and she had nothing to be ashamed of. She could pay her rent with a clean conscience. As far as Dr. Jefferies, he allowed her five sick days a year; until now she hadn't used any.

That month came and went without further incident. Towards the end of the next month Jackie found herself in similar financial circumstances. After a long sleepless night worrying about money and how to survive, she gave in to her alter ego, and made another deal to trade virtue for ideals. It wasn't a long fight, Jackie had been thinking about it for a whole month, waiting for the opportunity to reassert her new individualism.

The last Friday of the month Jackie wore a blue print dress with an empire waistline, covered with small lavender and white flowers, and a long overcoat. It was getting colder and the weather man was calling for rain. Of course she wore her lucky pearl necklace with matching earrings. She kept looking at her watch all day waiting for five o'clock.

She called a taxicab and had it pick her up at exactly five and take her directly to the Biltmore. Her heart was pounding so hard in her chest she was sure the cab driver could hear it. When they arrived at the Biltmore, Jackie had the driver go around the block one more time while she calmed herself down. The door man opened the cab door while she was paying the driver; he wasn't the same one that was on duty the day of her previous visit. She was pleased.

She entered the lobby of the Biltmore with more surety and went directly to the lounge with a distinct air of confidence.

Jackie surveyed the crowd in the lounge. It seemed busier than on her last visit. The tuxedo wearing piano player was busy playing a country song and the buffet was filled with freshly prepared foods.

Jackie deliberately hesitated on the top step knowing the male visitors would be looking at her and making sexist comments to one another. She went directly to the table she was sitting at when she met Phil. She sat down with her purse next to her on the same chair. This time when the waiter asked if he could get her something from the bar she did not hesitate.

"Yes, please, I would like a glass of Zinfandel."

The waiter nodded that he understood and retreated to the serving station.

Jackie sat quietly and listened to the music, hoping for someone to join her. Her drink came and still she was alone. She had just enough money to pay for her drink and a cab ride home. She decided at least she would fill up on the goodies before she left. If she didn't go home hungry at least it would make the trip worth while.

The buffet table was crowded. Jackie stood quietly waiting for her turn at the sausages, they were her favorite meat. After filling her plate, quite adequately, she looked disparagingly at the strawberry-filled tarts. Feeling confident that she had her money's worth, Jackie made her way back to her table.

"Excuse me, ma'am. I don't mean to interrupt your evening, but I noticed you had forgotten your utensils so I took the liberty of bringing you some."

Jackie looked up to see a man about her age standing before her. He was wearing a three-buttoned, navy-blue suit, a pink and white paisley tie and gold cuff links.

"Why, thank you," said Jackie, "I was preoccupied and hadn't realized I had forgotten them."

"May I join you or are you waiting for your date?"

"Oh, my, no I'm not waiting for anyone, and I would be pleased if you would sit down."

The young man was drinking a domestic beer from a bottle. That should have sent a signal to Jackie, but it didn't. Jackie was unfortunately naive about men and the whole bar scene as well.

"My name is Jeff," he said as he stuck out his hand for her to shake, "what's yours?"

"Jackie will do just fine." She placed her hand in his and he shook it vigorously.

His aggressive handshake was another missed signal; Jackie was new at the game, and would have to make mistakes in the learning process.

"Well, Jackie, do you come here often, or are you a guest of this fine establishment?" Jeff asked as he sat down across from Jackie.

"I work just around the corner, and I came by for a drink before going home. How about you, what brings you to our fair city?"

"Computers, Jackie, computers. I work for a small company that makes computers. I'm going to be the salesman of the year this year, yes sir, computers. Can't live without them."

"I see," said Jackie getting caught up in his enthusiasm, "you must be an awfully good salesman to be the best in your company."

"Well, lady, I'm not the best yet, but I will be by the end of the year. I've got what it takes to be successful," said the braggadocios Jeff.

"And just what that might be?" Jackie asked sincerely.

"Drive, intensity, enthusiasm, you name it and I've got it." Jeff answered as he downed the rest of his beer and held the bottle up over his head so the waiter would bring him another of the same.

Jackie was taken back by the rush of Jeff's personality. She sat quietly and ate her buffet while Jeff extolled his virtues. The waiter brought Jeff his beer.

"This is all very nice," Jackie finally got a word in, "you must be very successful." Jackie was doing some probing of her own.

"Well, I've only been with them for six months, but I've got my future all planned out." Jeff tilted his head back and slugged down half his bottle.

"Well, I work as a receptionist for a dentist." Jackie was trying to lay down the groundwork for sympathy.

"Great job for a woman. I don't think I've ever seen a man receptionist. Women have a natural talent for answering the phone and talking to people, don't you think?"

Jackie was missing all the signals. She would eventually look back on this meeting with great regret.

"I just love piano music," Jackie said trying to

change the subject. "Don't you find it relaxing?"

"It's okay I guess. When I was a kid my mother made me take piano lessons, and I learned to hate the piano."

"I wish my career was going as well as yours seems to be." Jackie was trying to get the conversation back on track. "I barely make enough money to pay my rent."

"You'd never know it to look at you, you look great." Jeff said as he waved his empty over his head again. "Maybe you should try sales, you have a pretty face and a good personality."

The waiter brought him his beer, Jeff paid him and still hadn't bothered to ask Jackie if she wanted another drink. The waiter did.

"Another glass of wine for the lady?"

Jackie hesitated thinking she may have to pay for it and was counting the change in her purse just in case.

"Yes, thank you."

"Put that on my bill, will you, buddy?" Jeff addressed the waiter.

"Of course, sir."

Jackie felt a breath of relief. She got her drink, now, if she could direct Jeff's attention to her needs she would be ahead of her plan.

"Well, Jeff, the dentist I'm working for is retiring this month. I'm going to be out of work and I won't have enough money to pay my rent." Jackie thought injecting a small white lie may add drama to the situation, and started to cry for extra effect.

It didn't work. Jeff acted as if he hadn't heard a word she said.

"Excuse me, but I've got to go shake hands with a friend, I'll be right back." With that Jeff got up and went to the men's room.

Jackie felt the frustration of the situation and started to cry for real. She wasn't getting anywhere. What was she going to do?

She decided to just leave before Jeff got back and forget about the disaster she was living through. Too late, Jeff returned.

"I've got a good idea, Jackie, let's go somewhere where its quieter and we can talk without interference."

Jackie finally felt she was getting somewhere. "Sure," she said and gulped down her glass of wine.

Jeff took her by the hand and lead her to the elevator. I've got wine in my room, it's a complimentary bottle," he said, "that way we don't have to pay five dollars a glass."

The elevator stopped at the third floor and the pair got out. Jackie was getting the feeling of being rushed. Jeff was out of the elevator door and down the hall before she was out of the elevator.

"Right this way," he said and held the door open for her. It was his first attempt at manners.

The room was nice, small with one king size bed, an entertainment unit with a TV and stereo. While Jackie looked around the small room and remembered the luxury suite Phil had, Jeff went to the small refrigerator in the room and opened a carafe of white wine.

"I hope you like the vintage," he said, "it's all they have." He handed her a water glass filled with the vinegar-like tasting fluid, kept one for himself, and held it up for a toast.

"Here's to good times."

Jeff tapped his glass to Jackie's and drank his wine

straight down. Jackie took a small sip and made a sour face.

Jeff, having finished his wine placed the empty glass on the shelf and grabbed Jackie. He pulled her close and started kissing her neck and the top of her breasts.

"Take off your jacket," Jeff ordered Jackie as he began to loosen his slacks.

Jackie was lost in the confusion. "What are you doing?"

"You know damn well what I'm doing," he said.

Jackie stood there and watched in amazement as Jeff disrobed in seconds kicking his garments all over the place and stood in front of her in only his argyle socks.

"What?" was the only thing Jackie had time to say before Jeff started undressing her. He wasn't taking time to unzip or unbutton, just pull and stretch. When he finally had Jackie down to her bra and panties, he pulled her panties down to her knees, rolled her over on her stomach and mounted her doggy style.

In a matter of seconds the whole ordeal was over. Jeff got up and went to the bathroom to clean off. Jackie sat on the edge of the bed in utter amazement. Even on Harry's worst days, there had never been an episode to match this one.

Jeff came out of the bathroom and threw her a hand towel. "Don't leak on the bed," he commanded.

Jackie made a feeble attempt to wipe off the dribble from her sexual encounter.

"What about me?" she demanded.

"What do you mean, 'what about me,' you got it didn't you, that's why you came with me to my room, isn't it?"

Jackie started to cry and get dressed. "No, no, this isn't right." Jackie cried out. "It isn't supposed to be like this."

Jackie was dressed, putting her shoes on. "And what about my rent money, you said you were going to help me pay my rent."

"What!" hollered Jeff loud enough to be heard all the way down in the lounge. "Was this about money? Are you telling me you expect to be paid for your services? You didn't tell me you were a god-damned hooker. If you had I would have picked out a better fuck."

Jeff was unloading rage and venom at Jackie. She had never had anyone speak to her like that before and was rightly sacred.

"Here, bitch," Jeff continued to holler and threw a fifty dollar bill at her, "now get the hell out of my room and if I ever see you in this hotel again I'm going to call the police and have you arrested."

Jackie picked up the money and shoved it in her purse. Then she made a dash for the door and left the still naked, still ranting Jeff in the middle of the room.

Jackie put her overcoat on in the elevator while going down. When she got to the lobby she didn't stop to find a cab--she walked instead.

It was late, Jackie didn't know how late, and she didn't care. It was getting colder, a blowing misty rain was splashing against her cheeks. The cold was bitter reality. Just then Jackie needed reality. She cried as she walked, but the mist had her face wet and the tears didn't show.

Jackie walked for hours not knowing where she

was going, and not caring. Finally when she had cried enough, and was wet and cold enough she knew she should go home.

Jackie had wandered many blocks from the downtown area. When she looked up to get her bearings she noticed she was far away from the tall buildings and street-lights.

Feeling uncomfortable where she was, Jackie began to walk faster. The faster she walked the more paranoid she became, hearing sounds and seeing shadows.

She saw a traffic light, a street light and a store with people in it across the street. Jackie stepped off the curb in the middle of the block to the safety of the lights, caught her heel on the broken curb and fell. She hollered when she went down. She fell face forward, skinned the palms of her hands, broke the heel on her shoe, and badly bruised her leg.

Jackie took both her shoes off, placed them in her coat pocket and limped over to Green's Twenty Four Hour Deli; where she could wash off, get some hot coffee, and plan her next move.

6   RANDOM ACT OF KINDNESS

Joe pulled up to the curb in front of the same apartment building he had stopped in front of earlier that same day to let Jackie out. Taking the small brown bag with the newly repaired shoe with him, he made his way to the front of the building stopping in front of the row of mail boxes near the door. Reading down the line he found the only "Jackie," a Jackie Jones living in apt. 2-B.

There wasn't a buzzer to ring like there is in many apartments, so he tucked the bag under his arm and trotted up the stairs. Apt. 2-B was the second door on the right. He hesitated and listened for sounds of life coming from behind the door. Joe glanced down at his watch, it was past two pm. He knocked gently, but firmly. Joe wasn't one to go pounding on other people's doors.

Joe waited for thirty seconds or so and knocked again. He heard some sounds coming from inside.

"Who is it?" Asked a sleepy voice from the other side.

"It's me, Joe the cab driver. Are you the lady I drove home last night?"

The voice didn't answer. There was a rattling of chains, and the sound of a dead bolt coming to life.

The door opened a crack.

A bloodshot, blue eye peered out.

"Oh, hi," said Jackie, a bit surprised, but otherwise happy to see Joe. "Come in, please. Can I pour you some orange juice, or get you a glass of water or something?" Jackie was wearing a night-shirt with a picture of Mickey Mouse on it, nothing else.

Joe entered the small, but neat and clean apartment. Jackie escorted him over to the table where he sat down. Jackie went over to the refrigerator and took the juice jar out of the refrigerator and placed it on the table. Joe noticed that other than the juice jar, a pizza box was the only thing he saw in Jackie's refrigerator. He felt sorry for her and more proud of himself for having taken the time to help her.

"No, thank you. I just stopped by to drop this off." And Joe handed Jackie the bag.

"Well I know it's not my birthday, what is it?" she said squeezing the bag. "My shoe, you brought me back my shoe, I remember, I left it in your cab." Jackie dumped the contents of the bag on the table and out fell a complete shoe.

"You fixed it!" She squealed with delight. "How nice of you. How much do I owe you? I'm afraid I can't afford much." Jackie added hurriedly.

"Not a thing, miss Jackie, it's on the house," Joe said smiling ear to ear. "Doing nice things for other people always makes me feel good inside."

"Why, aren't you a dear." Jackie got up, went around behind Joe and gave him a big bear hug.

Joe blushed. Jackie was pretty, even when she wasn't dressed up, he thought to himself, and she smelled better than fresh biscuits.

"I guess I'd better be going," Joe said as he backed up from the table.

"No, please don't go." Jackie said in a pleading voice. "I'd like to pay you something for your trouble. These are good shoes and it would cost me a lot to replace them."

"Naw, that's all right," Joe said proudly. "I was glad to do it."

"Please, I know what I can do, I can cook you dinner. What time do you go on duty tonight?"

"I go on from five to two a.m. tomorrow morning. Saturday is always a good night, especially in foul weather like this."

"Okay then, lunch tomorrow. You don't work on Sunday do you?"

Joe was starting to blush. "No, ma'am, I don't usually work on Sunday, but I really didn't do this expecting to get paid, or to receive a reward of any kind."

"Good, then you're surprised.... Look, Joe, I don't mean to be pushy. If you don't feel comfortable with my invitation I understand." Jackie, dropped her chin to the floor and gave Joe a lost puppy dog look.

Jackie quit smiling and backed around the table. Joe felt as if he needed to defend himself.

"Well, it's just that, well, I usually change Felix's cat box, do my wash, and generally clean the house on Sunday." Joe knew how terribly lame his reasoning must be sounding to Jackie. It almost made no sense to himself. "It's the only free time I have," he added, hoping to sound credible.

"I see, well thanks anyway, Joe." Jackie's voice was as low as her chin.

Joe walked over to the door, put his hand on the knob, and felt a tickle in his throat. He stopped, turned around and said, "I'll tell you what. If you don't mind coming to my house and helping me use up a whole lot of left-overs, it's a deal. I'll even send a cab to pick you up around two. How's that for a compromise?"

"Deal!" said Jackie, and ran around the table to kiss Joe on the cheek.

"Now, I've got a lot of food at my place, and being by myself I don't organize my kitchen very good, but I'm sure I've got anything you can want."

Joe left and heard Jackie locking the door behind him. He smiled to himself, looked at his watch and figured he had just about an extra hour to go grocery shopping before he had to go to work. After seeing what little food Jackie kept in her refrigerator he knew she couldn't even afford to make him lunch.

Joe usually kept little food in the house, too. Normally he would cook a roast or chicken on Sunday and then pick at it all week long. Other than a few odd cans, some of which had been in the cupboard since Martha died, Joe didn't keep many groceries in the house at all.

Joe decided to go back to the shopping center near his house and visit the local grocery store. It was an old grocery store, but Joe knew every one that worked there, and they made him feel right at home.

Normally Joe just carried a small red basket for the

few things he bought; that day he pushed a cart. He started with a loaf of whole wheat bread, dinner rolls, two cans of corn, two cans of peas, a whole chicken; then he decided to add a whole cut-up chicken, a three pound roast, a two pound slab of ham, and a package of hamburger in case Jackie wanted to make meat-loaf. For drinks he grabbed a six pack of diet soda and a six pack of regular soda. Joe didn't drink alcohol of any kind; he had gone on a drinking binge when Martha died but that lasted only a year. Joe looked around to see if there was anything else he might need. There was; butter, lettuce for a salad, a large yellow onion, a low calorie ranch dressing, a bunch of fresh cut flowers, and an angel food cake for dessert. Angel food cake was one of Joe's favorites.

Joe paid the bill and hurried home to put the things away before they spoiled. The flowers he placed in what used to be Martha's favorite vase and placed them in the center of the dining room table. Felix jumped up to check them out.

"Now, Felix," yelled Joe, "those are for company, don't you go knocking anything over. Do you hear? We are having a young woman over tomorrow who is down on her luck and I want you to be nice to her."

Joe looked around the house. Nothing seemed to be out of order. It had been a month since Joe had dusted or run the vacuum cleaner. "You know Felix," Joe said to the cat as he picked him up and cradled him in his arms, "sometimes I forget just how good we have it, then I run up on some misfortunate person, and it gives me pause to say thanks."

Felix just purred in agreement.

Jackie wasn't the first person Joe had brought

home to feed. There had been four others since Martha had died; and dozens while she was alive. All the rest had been men and all were during the bitter cold of winter. Most of them were homeless, some of them were drifters, but they were all cold and hungry. Because Martha was prone to be jealous, even though Joe had always been faithful, Joe only brought men home.

Joe had come from a very poor family and it wasn't unusual for his family to miss meals, especially the week rent came due. Joe and Martha would regularly donate their time on holidays to feed the poor at soup kitchens. Once Martha said to Joe, "Land's sake, Joe, most people bring home stray dogs, you come home with stray people."

"Do you want me to stop?" Joe would ask Martha.

Martha would give Joe a big bear hug and tell him he had a heart as big as his taxicab. It was the hug Jackie had given Joe when he returned her shoe that prompted the invitation and invoked the pleasant memory of Martha.

Joe looked at his watch; it was almost four. "I've got to gas up, Felix, watch the house for me while I'm gone. I won't get home until tomorrow morning-early."

Joe put Felix down on the counter and locked the door behind him. Felix made a dash to his spot in the bay window, as he always did, to watch Joe leave.

Jackie had slept in that same day until well past noon. Normally Jackie was an early riser, but with her luck going south on her and skills with men a disgrace, she found herself spending more time sleeping and worrying than usual.

Jackie sat at her kitchen-dining-room table and poured herself another glass of watered down orange juice. She looked at the shoe on the table that Joe had repaired and returned. It really was an expensive shoe, eighty dollars on sale.

She allowed her mind to freely drift back to the evening before when she met Joe in the diner. She remembered walking up to him and, noticing how kind he looked, trying not to laugh as the steam from his coffee fogged his glasses. The only reason she approached Joe was because she saw his cab when he drove up and was hoping to con him out of a free ride.

The thought of 'conning' someone was repulsive to Jackie. But she had done it, and to a nice man. She tried to rationalize to herself that she didn't steal anything from Joe. After all he was going home anyway and was just giving her a lift. Having her shoe fixed showed how very thoughtful he was. Harry would never do anything like that for anyone except himself. She decided fixing Joe dinner was the least she could do, and besides it helped her to alleviate the feeling of guilt.

Jackie rinsed out the juice glass and made her way to the bathroom. She turned on the tap in the tub and added a liberal amount of fragrance to the bubbles. Jackie did her best thinking while under the influence of hot bubbles.

She disrobed and looked longingly at the nasty bruise at the top of her thigh and noticed a small one on the back of her calf of the same leg. The scrape on her hand was almost gone. She didn't remember falling down that hard, but she must have.

Jackie turned off the water and stepped in.

"Ouch, ooh-ooh ouch!" Jackie yelled and stepped back out. She had forgotten to test the water and it was very hot. The water half filled the tub, the bubbles filled the rest. Jackie got her razor, placed a new blade in the head and carefully tip-toed into the still hot water. She sat on the cold porcelain rim of the tub and dangled her feet in the slowly cooling water while she shaved her legs.

Jackie remembered back when she had gone into pre-op to have her baby, a nurse shaved her pubic area. Jackie would look at herself in the mirror and fantasize about her hairless sexuality. She would think of herself as a young virgin once again; only this time it would not be Harry she would give herself to.

Jackie liked the clean look, and except for a small patch of hair along the top of her pubic line, continued to shave herself. Deep down inside she knew it was only because she had a reason to touch herself.

By the time she was done shaving her legs and other parts, the water had cooled just enough to allow her to slide her entire body under the bubbles and into the perfumed water. At first the hot water on her bruises stung. Then she enjoyed the stress relieving qualities of the hot bath. What was she going to do about money? She needed to go back to the lounge and this time be more selective about whom she allowed to sit down, that's for sure.

She decided the best thing she could do was avoid the Biltmore, just in case she ran into that idiot, Jeff, again. "Well there are a lot of other hotels in town. I'll just have to start fresh." Jackie thought to herself.

"What the hell are you doing to yourself?" Jackie shouted out to the non-responsive walls. "You're justifying taking money from men for sex. You're nothing but a cheap tramp, you-you Jezebel you." Jackie tried to cry but she could not. Deep down inside she knew she was doing what she really wanted to do, and besides, she didn't ask the men for money, she took it because they were being kind to her and it wouldn't be Christian like to turn down charity.

Jackie tried to wash her bruise but it was really sore. She knew she would have to give it time to heal before dating anyone else. It was the right thing to do she rationalized. Jackie was truly scared deep down inside. She had fallen from grace in her own mind, and was looking for a way to justify her landing.

Jackie washed her hair and felt much better. She dried off and put her night shirt back on. Her still moist body formed a perfect outline through the thin cotton. Looking at her it was easy to see why Mickey was smiling.

Jackie stood before her clouded bathroom mirror with a pair of scissors and began to trim the split ends from her still wet hair. Jackie had been trimming her own hair since she was a teen-ager. The only time she ever had her hair professionally done was when she got married.

Satisfied she had done a good job, Jackie put the scissors down and went to her small bedroom to get dressed. She chose a familiar combination; skin tight blue-jeans, one of Harry's old loose fitting flannel shirts, and moccasins. After following her normal dressing ritual she noticed it was late in the day and decided it would be best if she stayed home.

Jackie opted to use the remainder of the day to do the wash. She gathered together all her dirty clothes, stripped the bed and grabbed the soiled towels.

Carefully she placed her sheets on top of the table, then put the rest of her dirty laundry in the middle, folded the ends to the center and tied the entire bundle like a bandana.

Normally Jackie washed her clothes on Saturday morning. The Washateria was on the corner. She didn't like to go there after dark, even though it was well lit. Each washer took one dollar and the dryer was fifty cents for fifteen minutes. It usually took Jackie five or six dollars to do her weekly laundry. Today, however, she had a different plan.

* * * * *

Joe turned on his two-way radio, "Base, this is cab fifty-four checking in for my shift."

"Hello, Joe."

"Hello, Marty. How does it look for tonight?"

"Sid is out sick. It's his kidneys again. Other than that we have a full crew."

"I'm going down to the bus station, Marty. I'll call you if I snag anything."

The two bus stations were across the street from one another. The bars didn't start letting out until one in the morning. Joe didn't like bars. It wasn't because drinkers weren't good tippers, because they were. It was just that drunks had a habit of throwing up in his cab or passing out and he would end up giving them a free ride home. Once a drunk got sick in Joe's cab and it took two days to get the smell out. Joe lost a lot of money.

Joe's first fare that night was a soldier home on leave for the Thanksgiving holiday. He was a nice young man, very polite, Joe thought. Dispatch then called Joe to go to County General and pick up a man who was getting discharged a day early and needed a ride home.

The rest of the night was pretty uneventful. Joe liked it that way. After his last call, just after two the next morning, Joe ventured over to Green's Deli for his usual cup of Java before calling it a night.

"Coffee, Joe?"

"Don't I always, Mike?"

Mike brought Joe his cup of coffee down to his regular spot at the bar.

"That was some good looking lady you took home from here last night Joe."

"Yeah, she is. Does she come in here much, Mike?"

"No, Joe, last night was the first time I ever saw her before. Why?"

"Just curious that's all."

Mike returned to the far end of the bar and filled just washed salt and pepper shakers. Joe picked up an old copy of the newspaper and read the sports section while he waited for his coffee to cool.

There was a young couple sitting in a booth holding hands, staring lovingly in one-another's eyes. The rest of the deli was empty. It was probably a combination of the cold weather and the coming holiday.

7   A NEW BEGINNING

Sunday arrived. At five minutes before two Jackie heard a knock at her door. The peep hole was broken so she asked, "Who's there?"

"It's me, miss Jackie, Joe."

There was a rattling of chains and the door opened.

"My, my, Jackie, don't you look nice today."

Jackie's complexion was clean and her dark features were pronounced against her soft, untanned skin; a swipe of pink lipstick and a hint of eyeliner were all the cosmetics she wore. She was wearing a simple lavender sun dress over a white blouse with three-quarter length sleeves.

"Please come in, Joe. I'll just be a minute."

Joe entered and waited for Jackie to return from her bedroom.

"Joe, I have a small favor to ask," Jackie shouted from the back so Joe could hear.

"Sure, miss Jackie, what is it?"

"Well, Joe," Jackie said as she returned, "the washer and dryer downstairs are out of order, and I was wondering if you would mind me using yours while I cooked dinner?"

"Of course not."

"I was hoping you would say that, I have a bundle there in the corner. Would you mind helping me with it?"

"I'd be honored to, Miss Jackie."

"And just one more small thing you could do for me Joe."

"If I can, what is it?"

"Please quit calling me Miss Jackie. Jackie is just fine. When you say Miss Jackie, it makes me feel old and feeble. Okay?"

"I'm sorry," Joe said somewhat embarrassed. He picked up the bundle of dirty clothing and headed out the front door. Jackie followed, locking the door behind them.

"This time you can sit up front with me," Joe told Jackie after placing the laundry in the trunk.

"Why thank you, Joe."

It was a quiet ride back to Joe's home. Traffic was light so they made the trip in about twenty minutes.

The first thing Jackie saw when they pulled up in the driveway was Joe's cat, Felix, at his sentry post in the bay window.

"My word what a beautiful cat. Is it yours Joe? Does he have a name?"

Joe went to the trunk and retrieved his cargo. "That's my buddy, Felix."

Jackie had her hand on the window and Felix was pawing at her through the glass.

"This way, Jackie."

Joe led the way to the side door that opened into the kitchen. The house had a front door, but Joe couldn't remember the last time he used it. Even when Martha was alive they used the side door. It just seemed like the thing to do. Whenever they went grocery shopping they placed the groceries on the kitchen shelf. If the weather was bad Joe would take off his shoes and leave them by the back door to dry. The washer and dryer were in a small room just off the kitchen.

Joe opened the side door and stepped back to let Jackie in first.

"Oh, Joe, isn't this nice."

Felix was standing on the counter in his position as the formal greeter. Jackie picked him up as soon as she saw him, cradled him in her arms and began stroking him.

"He's your friend for life now, Jackie."

Joe placed the basket filled with soiled laundry on top of the washer.

"I might as well give you the cook's tour."

It didn't take long for Joe to show Jackie around the small two bedroom duplex. Jackie noticed his bed was made and there were pictures of Martha on the night stand as well as on the wall over the sofa.

"Joe, I'm really impressed at how clean and neat your house is. Do you hire someone to help you?"

"No, I don't. Felix and me don't make too much of a mess, so it's not too hard to keep up."

"Why don't you see if there's sports on the tube you want to watch, and I'll find my way around the kitchen." Jackie took control of the situation without realizing it. Her cheerful smile and soft-spoken way helped to ease the situation.

"There's lots of food in the refrigerator," Joe said opening the door to the cold spot, "and the pots and pans are in that cupboard over there."

"Can I get you a beer or a soda?" Jackie asked.

"I quit drinking after Martha died. I don't have any beer, but there are plenty of cold sodas in the fridge. I didn't know what kind you liked to drink so I bought two kinds."

"Do me a favor, Joe. You go watch TV while I reconnoiter the kitchen."

Joe shrugged his shoulders and went into the living room with Felix hot on his heels.

Jackie spent the next five or ten minutes rummaging around the kitchen looking to see where everything was kept. Then she went through the refrigerator and freezer to see what there was to cook. She was amazed at the variety of food available. Then she smiled to herself, realizing that Joe had bought all this for her visit. To Jackie, that simple act of kindness showed her Joe was a caring person. Someone who was more concerned about someone else's feelings than their own. A rare quality indeed, Jackie thought.

Joe sat in his recliner with Felix on his lap, listening to the clatter of pots and pans and the sound of the electric can opener. Finally, his curiosity got the best of him and he found his way back to the kitchen.

"I forgot to change Felix's litter box," Joe said looking around at all the pans and bowls filled with food in different stages of completion.

"I already did that," Jackie replied. "I had to move the box to get to the washer and dryer. I remembered you said Sunday was your day to change the box, so I thought I'd help out. I hope you don't mind?"

As if in disbelief, Joe went to the utility room to check. While there he recognized the sheets to his bed on top of the washer.

"What are you doing with my sheets?" he said in a manner that reflected an invasion of privacy.

Jackie chose to ignore his mood.

"Washing them, silly. Remember, you told me Sunday was the day you did laundry and changed Felix's litter box? I stripped the bed and gathered up the towels and dirty clothes from the hamper in the bathroom."

Joe just stood there red faced and embarrassed.

"I didn't invite you over to anything more than cook us both a good meal. I didn't expect you to be doing all these other things."

"And I'm doing just that, now go back and watch TV. Dinner is almost done." Jackie flashed Joe a friendly smile and shooed him away.

"Good, then I can set the table," Joe said as he retreated from the kitchen. And he did.

Joe opened the china hutch and took out dishes that hadn't been used for almost ten years. He held the plates close to his face looking for dust, then as if out of habit, brushed the plates off with his sleeve. He started placing the silverware but couldn't remember which side the forks went on so he put everything on the right side. Joe was right handed.

Just as Joe was placing the fancy cloth napkins Jackie walked in with the salad items.

"My goodness, Joe, what a beautiful setting." She went to the flowers in the center of the table and smelled them. "Are these for me, or your other girl friend?"

Joe looked embarrassed, he felt his face flush.

"Whenever Martha and me had Sunday dinner together I always brought her flowers."

Then it was Jackie's turn to get embarrassed. "You miss her a lot, don't you, Joe?"

Joe smiled and nodded, his eyes glistened with tears that did not fall.

"Well, Joe, you just sit down at the head of the table and allow me to bring in the rest of the dinner."

Jackie cooked the pot roast complete with potatoes and carrots and plenty of gravy. She made rolls and the smell of freshly cooked food filled the house for the first time since Martha passed. Joe bowed his head and said grace. "Lord, thank you for the food and some one to help eat it. Amen."

"Joe, I've got a meat loaf in the oven. It's for you later in the week. All you will need to do is heat it up. The rest of the food you bought I put in the freezer so it wouldn't spoil."

"Thank you, Jackie, that was very kind of you. I couldn't help but notice your refrigerator looked hungry. Why don't you take the meat loaf home with you. There will be plenty of left-overs here for me and Felix."

"Absolutely not!" Jackie almost snapped back. Then seeing the hurt look on Joe's face she recanted, "How about I take the chicken instead? That is, if you don't mind? I really prefer poultry to red meat."

A smiling Joe said, "You got it."

The rest of the meal went quietly, each person not wanting to offend the other. Then when Jackie got up to clear the table Joe took control.

"Jackie, there's angel food cake in the refrigerator

and some vanilla ice cream in the freezer. It's my favorite dessert, will you have some with me?"

The thoughtful gesture touched Jackie, she wasn't used to someone else caring for her well-being.

"Just a small piece, Joe, a girl has to watch her weight these days; you never know who's watching."

Joe couldn't help being nosey, being a cab driver it was an occupational hazard.

"How much do you pay for rent?" he asked abruptly.

Jackie was taken by surprise and stuttered.

"Well, Joe, the first two months were free, after that it's six hundred dollars a month."

"Does that include utilities?"

"Heat and water, and garbage collection. Why do you ask?"

"It just seems to me a young woman like you working in a dentist office can't be making a whole lot of money, that's all."

The direction of the conversation caught her completely off guard and she began to cry. At first Jackie sat there with the hint of a tear in the corner of her eye trying to be brave. Alas she could no longer hold back the flood of anxiety and sadness and left her crying for the bathroom where she closed and locked the door. Joe followed apologizing for upsetting her. He stood outside the bathroom door listening to the painful crying sounds one makes when truly hurt. His first impulse was to knock on the door and ask her to..., to what? He went back to the table and finished his cake.

Almost twenty minutes went by before Jackie made her way back to the table. The air was thick with tension and regret.

"Please take me home."

Joe was choked with emotion. His face was red with exasperation from the results of his boldness. It was time for him to be noble.

"Certainly, I will. But first indulge an old man if you will."

"Joe, you're not old, but I do feel as though I have overstayed my welcome. I really must go."

"Now, see, that's what I mean. You're still welcome here, please, sit down. Have a cup of coffee with me, then I'll take you home."

Joe went to the kitchen without waiting for a response from Jackie, plugged in the coffee maker, then returned to the dining room table.

"It takes four or five minutes, and fresh coffee happens. I hope you drink coffee?"

"Some, I'm not a big coffee drinker, but it's okay."

"I've got some hot chocolate if you'd rather have that," Joe said patronizing her.

"That's okay, coffee is fine," came a terse response.

"With marshmallows," Joe said smiling ear to ear.

Jackie saw the effort Joe was making and couldn't help but to break out in a smile of her own.

"Chocolate would be great, and with two marshmallows."

The two sat and exchanged stories about their spouses. Joe told kind and loving stories about Martha. His love for her was evident in the respectful way he spoke about her. Jackie was far more unkind in her description of Harry and the financial mess he left her with. She spoke ever so briefly of her dead child and the scar she was sure she would carry for life.

"I don't want you to go crying to the bathroom

again, Jackie, but how do you supplement your income enough to pay rent?"

Jackie certainly wasn't about to tell Joe she was looking for contributions from strangers. Jackie refused to own up to the fact that she was selling sexual favors for rent. After all she still considered herself a Christian lady.

"I had some money left from selling my furniture and things Joe, but it's almost gone."

There was a break in Jackie's voice, her eyes filled with tears.

"The chocolate is too hot."

Joe knew better. One thing he learned on his job was to judge people. Jackie was good people, but he could tell she was hurting. He also knew Jackie didn't fit into her environment. She was cut from a different bolt of cloth than the people who surrounded her. Surely she would begin to take on the characteristics of her surroundings if there wasn't a positive change in her life.

"You know, Jackie, I've been having problems with arthritis lately, and this house is getting too much for me to handle. I was thinking about signing up for one of those retirement places, but they won't let me bring Felix."

"Oh, Joe, you don't want to go to a retirement home, that's no place for you. You wouldn't be happy there." Jackie immediately went into the mothering mode most women have.

Joe saw her take the bait and decided to try and gently reel her in.

"I know, Jackie, but keeping up a house this big is just more than I want to deal with."

"Why, Joe, if you need help I could come by

whenever, and help you with the chores if you'd like."

Joe had the conversation going in the direction he wanted, then like a good salesman he went for the close.

"I checked into a cleaning service. They only want fifty dollars each visit to come two afternoons a month to maintain minimum service. The money is okay, but I don't want strangers wandering around my house. Do you know what I mean?"

Jackie was doing some quick addition, two afternoons a month, one hundred dollars, not bad.

"Joe, you're right, you don't need strangers snooping around. I'd be glad to help you until you're feeling better."

"Well, Jackie," Joe said scratching his head, "I would much rather have you here than some drug dealer looking to steal my belongings. But I could only do it with a clear conscience if you let me pay you the going rate. Deal?"

"Deal, Joe," Jackie said excitedly as she hopped up and kissed him on the forehead.

Joe was once again red-faced, but smiling. He really didn't have all that much to do as far as house cleaning went, but then he really didn't like to dust or vacuum either. He figured Jackie would get her head straight in a couple of months and she would be gone. That was his way of helping someone else in need.

"Let me clear the dishes, and load the dishwasher. You and Felix go and relax in front of the TV."

Joe and Felix returned to the living-room and Jackie disappeared in the kitchen. It wasn't fifteen minutes later that Jackie joined Joe in the living-room, not to watch TV, but to vacuum and dust. Joe sat in quiet amazement and watched.

"I'm almost done here, then I'll make your bed and hang the clean towels and that's that."

Jackie had a renewed zest he hadn't seen before. He figured it was because she was helping herself by helping someone else. Joe was only a high-school graduate, but he knew people. After all, that's how he made his living.

"Joe, would you come here in the kitchen for a few minutes," Jackie said proudly, "I've got something I'd like to show you."

Joe got up out of his easy chair, Felix followed, and the two of them went into the kitchen.

"Look here," said Jackie as she opened the freezer compartment to the refrigerator, "I've made you some TV dinners, roast beef, potatoes and gravy and one roll each covered with plastic wrap. All you need to do is take one out and heat it on medium in your micro-wave for three minutes, and voila`, a hot, home-cooked meal."

Joe looked around in utter amazement, not only did the kitchen sparkle, but the air smelled fresh. He had lived with cat box odors so long he had become accustomed to the funky smell. Jackie was beaming with pride showing Joe what she had accomplished.

"My goodness, Jackie, I can't believe what I'm seeing. Not since Martha was alive did this kitchen look so good or smell so nice." And he went over to her and gave her a big hug.

She squealed in acceptance. Her days hadn't been going so well lately and it was nice to be genuinely appreciated for just being herself.

Joe looked her in the eye, smiled and said, "Now there's only one more thing to make this complete."

He reached into the freezer, retrieved the package of ground beef and cut up chicken, and handed them to her. "This is part of the deal also." Joe took out his wallet and handed Jackie five twenty dollar bills.

"But you don't have to pay me for today, and besides this is too much."

"The other cleaning service wanted me to pay up front, so you're no better or worse than they are. A deal is a deal."

Jackie wanted to make a fuss but she knew it wouldn't do any good, and besides, she knew she really needed the money and she didn't want to talk him out of it. She put the money in her blouse pocket and hugged Joe again, only this time, without thinking, she gave him a quick kiss on his lips.

"Take me home, Joe, before I start to cry again. You've made me a very happy person. I wish I had met you in school and not Harry."

8 WALK ON THE WILD SIDE

Joe carried Jackie's laundry to her door, but declined her offer to go in. They agreed that Jackie would go back to Joe's in two weeks to clean. Jackie went through the ritual of locking her door while Joe paused for a few extra seconds to make sure everything was all right.

Jackie was still on an emotional high. She had food for her freezer and in her stomach, and enough money in her pocket, along with her pay check to pay her rent for another month. Jackie sang to herself while she put her clothes in their proper drawers. Mentally she was adding up her pay with her new part time job. She took home a little more than two hundred and fifty dollars each week. It took two and a half paychecks to pay her rent and phone bill. That left one and a half checks to pay for her food, bus, cleaning and personal needs. It was a real close call each month. Jackie was especially thankful for the four times a year when she had an extra payday in the month.

What Jackie was really doing was seeing if she could make enough money on her own without having to subject herself to the whims of bar room Romeos to supplement her income.

Solid in the knowledge that she could, she sang louder to drown out the sounds of passing fire trucks. The sounds from the street were omnipresent but manageable. Then Jackie did as she had always done. She went to her closet and picked out the outfit she would wear to work the next day. Jackie was lucky, because she hadn't needed to buy any clothes, since she had plenty from her marriage. Buying new clothes or replacing them would be too costly for her current budget.

Jackie went to the refrigerator and poured herself a watered down glass of orange juice. She sat down at her small table, put her face in her hands and cried. She was tired, frustrated, emotionally drained, and more confused and afraid than she had ever been in her whole life.

She didn't like where she was living, but it was all she could afford. She liked her job all right, but it couldn't support her. She was aware of a new sensual side of herself she had never known before and she didn't know how to deal with it.

After the evening she spent with Phil at the Biltmore Jackie knew there was another side of her that existed; an intimate side, a side filled with passion and even lust. She could not ignore the feelings that stirred deep within her. Although the battle for her soul raged between her religious upbringing and her need for fulfillment, Jackie knew deep down that her unleashed sexuality could no longer be contained.

The next week at work was routine and uneventful. Jackie would get up at six fifteen each morning to get dressed for work. She decided by taking her bath at night she saved forty five minutes in the morning. She would catch the seven thirty bus on the corner and get to work by eight fifteen. The office didn't open officially until eight thirty so the timing was perfect.

On Wednesday she got an invitation to a bridal shower for one of her co-workers to be held in the Towers Hotel the Friday of the same week. Jackie wanted to go but was afraid she couldn't afford it. At the close of business that day she spoke to the bride-to-be.

"Tracy, I got your invitation to your shower...,"

"I'm so glad you can come," Tracy butted in, "it's a girls only night. Besides I have something special planned for entertainment. Anyway, there will be lots of food and an open bar, you'll have a blast."

"Why, yes, sure, I'd be glad to come." Jackie was having trouble accepting, but the promise of food and drink helped her make up her mind. "What should I wear?"

"Well, you know of course, the Towers is one of this city's finest hotels," Tracy was trying to sound important. "We rented a private dining room, so dress pretty, but not extravagant. You know, something you would wear on a first date to make a good impression, but not so nice you'd ruin it if you got lucky."

"I think I know just what you mean," Jackie said. "I'll see you Friday night around eight."

"Please, please don't be late, the entertainment will

be on time and I swear you won't want to miss it."

Tracy had only been working for Dr. Jefferies for about one year. She was what Jackie referred to as a dumb blonde. She had a squeaky voice and giggled a lot. Tracy spent most of her lunch time on the phone talking to her fiancee, Robert. Jackie almost always took her lunch to work; to save money and because they only had forty five minutes to eat. Except for a small container of yogurt, Tracy never ate lunch. She was paranoid about gaining weight.

Except for the fact that Tracy was five or six years younger than herself, Jackie didn't know a whole lot about her. The more Jackie thought about the bridal shower the happier she became. It would take her mind off of her problems and wouldn't cost her anything more than a small gift; Jackie had some antique silver candle holders she hated. All she had to do was wrap them up and give them as a present. They would do just fine. She smiled to herself for being so cunning.

Friday came and Jackie was extra busy that day. Tracy called in sick. Everyone knew she was having a party that night. No one was surprised.

Jackie wore a deep burgundy pant suit with a frilly white blouse to work. She couldn't afford to go home to get dressed and turn around to go back down town. The Towers were just a block past the Biltmore on the same street.

Jackie left work at her usual time that day and because the Towers were only twenty minutes away by bus she got there early. Jackie and Harry had driven past the Towers before, but they never had occasion to go there. When she arrived she went to the registration desk and asked which room the bridal shower would be held.

"It will be in the Williamsburg Room, ma'am, however that room won't be ready for another hour or so. Perhaps you would like to try our happy hour buffet. On Friday nights ladies drinks are half price."

"Thank you, I will. Which way to your lounge?" Jackie was showing more signs of being self assured.

"Past the elevators on your left, follow the hall to the end."

Jackie nodded and went down the hall. The carpet was thick dark green with gold threads. As she approached the lounge she heard the distinct sounds of a piano. "I wonder," she thought to herself, "if pianos are standard equipment with nice lounges?"

The bar was horseshoe shaped. The piano was near the entrance where there were small tables and chairs scattered around. Jackie looked around for a dance floor. There was none. A small table with food was along the wall between the piano and the bar. Jackie went to the buffet table first. She helped herself to Swedish meat balls, manicotti and meat sauce. There were carrot sticks and celery stalks; Jackie picked one of each.

There were only a few people sitting at the bar. Jackie sat at the table closest to the piano. A cute young waitress asked her for her drink order.

"I would like a glass of Zinfandel if you have it."

"Certainly, would there be anything else?"

Jackie nodded no, and hungrily attacked her plate of food. Before the waitress came back with her glass of wine, Jackie had gone back to the buffet table and was on her second plate.

"Is there anything you would like to hear?" the piano player asked Jackie as she sat down.

Jackie was embarrassed. She had her mouth full of food.

"Surely you have a favorite tune or song I might play for you."

"Well, actually there is," said Jackie regaining her composure. "Can you play Mac Arthur Park?"

Not only did the piano player know the tune, he also knew the lyrics and sang them beautifully.

Jackie sat motionless throughout the entire rendition. A tear came to her eye as she relived the last evening she had heard it.

The waitress came back to the table with another glass of wine.

"I'm sorry, miss," Jackie addressed the waitress, "I didn't order this."

"No, ma'am, it's from that gentleman at the bar."

Jackie glanced at her watch, six-thirty, "Tell him thank you."

She turned toward the bar, an elderly man in a navy-blue pin striped suit with a red paisley tie was holding his glass up as if in a toast and smiling. Jackie smiled back and turned her attention back to the piano player.

"Have you been playing the piano here long?"

"Almost every weekend for five years."

"Are there a lot of regulars who come here or are most of them from out of town?"

"Probably fifty-fifty. Why do you ask?"

"Do you know the man at the bar who bought me this drink?"

"I don't know his name, but he comes in all the time. He's a local, if that's what you mean."

The man at the bar made his way over to Jackie before she could finish her conversation with the piano player.

"Good evening, miss."

Jackie turned and smiled at her visitor. "Thank you for the glass of wine. It wasn't necessary of you to do that."

"May I sit down?" he asked. His voice was deep and resonent. He wasn't very tall, thinning hair, with a stocky build. He was impeccably dressed right down to his mother of pearl stick-pin.

"Please do."

The piano player continued playing the theme from 'Cats'.

"My name is Bradley, my friends call me Brad. I hope you'll be among them."

"I'm Jackie, Brad, how many friends do you have?"

"Everyone I lend money to, the ones I don't have other names for me."

"I beg your pardon?"

"I'm a banker, First State Savings and Loan." He handed her his card.

Jackie read the card, with raised gold print on a gray stock. "Bradley J. Clark, First Vice-president." It had his office number, his pager number, his car phone number and his home phone number on it.

"I'll be sure to call you if I need a loan. I see I would have a lot of numbers to choose from."

Bradley laughed and so did Jackie. It was a tension relieving type of laugh. She was giving him a serious once-over while he fumbled for some matches.

"You don't mind if I smoke do you?"

"Well, I...," Jackie tried to answer, but Bradley had taken a long cigar out of his inside pocket and was rolling it across a lit match. His bulbous cheeks imitated a feeding chipmunk as he puffed, filling the air around his head with a perfumed smoke.

"I like a good cigar, don't you?"

"Well, truthfully," Jackie said with a sound of arrogance, "no one around me smokes cigars."

Getting the message, like a bull in a china shop, Bradley decided to change directions. "What brings you to our fair city, Jackie?"

"Actually, I live here. I'm attending a friend's bridal shower in about an hour."

That wasn't the answer Bradley was hoping to hear.

"Excuse me, Jackie, I see one of my friends at the bar waving to me. He probably wants to borrow some money to pay his bar bill. Nice meeting you." And he scurried away.

Jackie smiled confidently to herself at the way she had handled the situation. Her first impulse was to put his business card in the ash tray, but instead put it in her purse. This was the first banker she had ever met, and who knew when one would come in handy.

Jackie picked up her purse and the wedding gift and headed for the powder room before looking for the Williamsburg room. She felt it would be safer to wait the last few minutes in the same room as the party; besides she thought she might be of some use in setting up the room.

Tracy had just arrived with the streamers and helium filled balloons.

"Hi, Tracy, need some help?"

"Why, Jackie, aren't you a dear. Why don't you set the card table over in this corner and we'll use it for the gifts. Do you think I'll get some?"

"I don't know, how many people did you invite?"

"Twenty, but I only expect fifteen to show."

Not more than five minutes went by when a young man, in his early twenties with long blond hair, blue eyes and a tuxedo, arrived.

"Tracy, he's gorgeous, but I thought there weren't going to be any men here."

"Oh, Jackie, he's important. He's the bartender."

The two girls laughed like two girls would on a sleep-over. The bartender asked where he should set up the bar.

"Over there at the end of the room away from the door would be nice," Tracy said.

"Which one of you two lovely ladies is the bride-to-be?" he asked.

"I wish it were me," said Jackie, "but it's her. She's Tracy and I'm Jackie. Who are you."

"I'm Rodney, but my friends call me 'Hot Rod'."

The two women broke out laughing once again and were joined by yet another woman. She was in her middle twenties and had very short blond hair that was heavily sprayed and combed straight up like a porcupine. She had a pierced nose and five earrings in one ear and six in the other.

"Jackie, I'd like you to meet Monica. She's my maid of honor."

"Greetings, Jackie. What can I do to help?"

More and more guests arrived until there were indeed fifteen, counting the guest of honor. Rodney had set up a very fine buffet line and a limited wet bar: lite beer, white wine, a whiskey blend and all kinds of soda.

Except for Tracy, Jackie didn't know anyone there. In fact, Jackie was the oldest, and that made her feel self-conscious. Most of the women were talking about sex with their boyfriends or husbands. Four of them were married and complained about the same old same old. Monica kept trying to make friends with Jackie, but Jackie thought Monica was somewhat of a flake so she kept her distance.

About and hour and a half into the event everyone had had something to eat and was at least on their fourth drink. Monica was on, who knows what Monica was on, but you could hear her all the way down to the ladies room. Rodney was very quiet. He kept the buffet table filled and all the requests for drinks. He was seen taking napkins with phone numbers and tucking them neatly in his tip jar.

Some of the women were openly smoking marijuana cigarettes and others were passing around a snifter and inhaling. Jackie stayed pretty much to herself. She kept looking at her watch, and had decided that as soon as Tracy opened the gifts, she would leave.

The party was getting louder by the minute. Tracy tapped her empty wine goblet with a spoon to get everyone's attention. Monica came up behind Jackie and held out a napkin with some small brownie looking cakes.

"Here try one," Monica said. Jackie was in the party mood, and although she wasn't a big chocolate eater, felt obliged to eat one.

"My goodness, Monica, these are very tasty."

"Oh, I'm so glad you like them. Take some more, I made a whole tray. They contain my very special ingredient." Then she laughed, "You won't find this recipe in Betty Crocker."

They were so good that Jackie ate four. After all, they were small and she didn't want to hurt Monica's feelings.

"Girls, girls," Tracy was hollering out to gain attention, "before we open the gifts I'd like you all to find a chair and sit down."

Everyone grabbed a chair and tried not to giggle.

Tracy continued, "Rodney, or should I say 'Hot Rod', before you go would you play the music I had you bring?"

The room was filled with boos, and someone started to chant, "We want Hot Rod, we want Hot Rod." Pretty soon all the girls were clapping and shouting. Jackie was beginning to feel light-headed, as if she had way too much to drink. She found herself joining in with the crowd.

Rodney produced a boom box and placed it on top of the bar, inserted a tape and turned up the volume. It was a hard rock instrumental. Then to everyone's surprise, except for Tracy's and Monica's, Hot Rod, began to dance his way to the front. He wasn't slow dancing, he was gyrating to the fast beat of the music. As he swung his hips forwards and backwards in front of his clapping and cheering crowd, he slowly began to take off his jacket. He swung it around in a circle over his head.

"More, more, take off more," they yelled. "We want to see more." The crowd was clapping to the music.

Hot Rod was wearing a tear away uniform. With one movement his shirt was off and on Tracy's lap. The second time around the room his pants and shoes were off and found their way to Jackie's lap; who turned bright red. She had never seen an adult film in her life, much less a male stripper.

Hot Rod was wearing the skimpiest of loin cloths. It was a small triangular shiny gold cloth in front with a thong tied in back. Hot Rod was dancing from girl to girl, showing off his tanned Adonis-like body.

The room was in pandemonium. Some of the girls started going into their purses and taking dollar bills out so they could stick them in Hot Rod's elastic waist band.

The music was loud and fast, the noise was deafening. Jackie was high as a kite. The room was spinning and she was yelling and looking for money to put in Hot Rod's golden jock strap.

When Hot Rod made it back around the room to where Jackie was sitting she took out her dollar to stick on his hip; just as she began to tuck it in he deftly swung to the front. Jackie was amazed and had to ask, in a very loud voice, "Why isn't it hard?"

Every one heard and the room broke out into laughter. Jackie didn't realize they were laughing at her.

"Are you sure its not hard?" Hot Rod asked.

Jackie was having much too much fun to be embarrassed, "Of course it's not hard, I can see it.""You can see through my cloth?" Hot Rod asked.

Jackie never looked up, she just kept staring at his crotch and nodding her head.

"Can you see it better now?" and with that he pulled his jock strap down to his thigh, and swung his limp instrument in front of her. "Can you blow it up for me?"

"Let me, let me!" Cries came from all around the room. Hot Rod danced over to the bride-to-be and in front of all the guest let her inflate his balloon. As Tracy took him in her mouth the circle of women tightened to get a better look; including Jackie, who was at first repulsed, but the more she watched, the hotter she got.

Hot Rod let Tracy finish him off and the intoxicated crowd cheered. As soon as the sex act was over he left and so did the crowd, never taking time to open the gifts.

"Just leave them on the table, Jackie. I'll put them in a box and take them home. Did you have a good time?"

"My Lord, Tracy, I've never in my life seen anything like that."

"Makes you hot just watching, doesn't it."

"My head is spinning so fast I just don't know what has gotten into me. I don't think I had that much wine."

"Did you eat any of Monica's brownies?" Tracy asked.

"Yes, four or five, I think."

Tracy laughed, and laughed. She walked over to Jackie and put her arm around her.

"Don't drive home right away. Those brownies were laced with marijuana. It shouldn't make you sick, but it's going to take awhile to come down."

Jackie was horny and high as a kite. She wanted to go sleep it off, but she was feeling too good and didn't want to waste it.

"Look, Tracy, I'm going back to the lounge and listen to the piano player for awhile, then I'll ride the bus home."

"I can give you a lift if you'd like, honest, I don't mind a bit."

Monica helped Tracy carry her still unopened gifts to the car and Jackie made her way back to the lounge. She took the wine glass she had been drinking out of all night and filled it with Sprite.

Jackie knew not to drink any more, and this would give her something to do while she sat and sobered up, or came down.

Jackie was incredibly high and had to brace herself several times against the wall to keep from falling. On her way back to the lounge she stopped in the lady's room and splashed cold water on her face; it seemed to help.

9 TWO FOR ONE

Jackie managed to find her way back to the lounge without spilling her soda. She sat at the first empty table she came to; not trusting her balance, she didn't want to walk any further than she had to.

Jackie had heard about male dancers, but had never seen one, and if Harry had been there... wow. Jackie laughed out loud thinking about how upset Harry would have been, the prude. Hot Rod had stood just inches in front of her, exposing himself, gyrating his body, and teasing her to the point where she thought she would have to go to the lady's room just to relieve herself, or do it right in front of everyone.

Jackie wanted Hot Rod. She wanted him to dance for her, she wanted him to stand right in front of her and tease her to the point of climax. She was jealous of Tracy. Tracy was a free spirit. Jackie wanted to be free.

The bar was almost full. Jackie looked at her watch; it was almost eleven-thirty. The piano player had a large bowl on top of his piano filled with money people had left as tips.

Jackie felt a hand on her shoulder and jumped with the start, almost overturning her drink.

"Whoa, now Jackie, it's only me, remember, Bradley?"

Jackie turned and faced the uninvited guest as he made his way around the small table.

"The banker, right?"

"Right. I thought you had some sort of formal engagement to attend this evening?"

"I did, and it's now over." Jackie was smiling and flirting with Bradley in a very coy way. She was so messed up with drugs and booze she didn't know what she was doing.

"Well now, pretty lady, you seem to be more relaxed now than when we first met earlier this evening." Bradley pulled his chair right up next to Jackie and put his hand on her thigh.

"Your hand doesn't belong there." Jackie said in a soft sensuous tone.

"Oh, really," said Bradley, "just where does it belong?"

Jackie sat looking directly in his face licking her lips and smiling. "Do you have a room here? I'll show you."

"Hell no, but I've got a Cadillac with a big back seat."

"Nope, no cars. I don't like cars." Jackie was playing with him.

"Now just suppose I got a room," said Bradley, "would I be needing a single bed or a double bed?"

"A king-sized bed," was Jackie's reply.

"Wait here, I'll be right back." And Bradley got up and left.

Jackie sat stirring her drink with her finger, then licking her finger. She was feeling no pain and acting a part she had never played before.

Bradley returned with a room key.

"Come on, Jackie, let's see what kind of a room we got for our money."

Bradley held out his arm and helped Jackie out of her chair. He was smiling from ear to ear. In the elevator on the way up to the room Bradley had his hand on Jackie's rear, patting it tenderly.

He was down the hall almost to the room before Jackie made it out of the elevator. To say he was excited with anticipation would be an understatement. Bradley opened the door to the room and let Jackie in first. "Do you want a drink or something?" he asked.

"No thank you, I've had more than I need already," said Jackie, her head spinning.

Bradley sat on the edge of the King-sized bed and patted it. "Is this enough room?" he asked with a wicked smile.

"It depends on how active you are," Jackie said as she rubbed her breasts through her dress.

That got Bradley turned on extra hot and he began getting undressed. Jackie watched.

"Aren't you going to get undressed? Or am I going to be the only one in bed tonight?" Bradley asked.

"It depends." Jackie was unbuttoning her blouse, in a sensuous teasing manner, slowly exposing her lacy bra and milk white breasts and playfully rubbing her already erect nipples.

"On what?" Bradley pleaded.

"Well, if I leave now, I can still catch the last bus home. If I wait I'm going to have to take the cab home. And the cab is more expensive."

"Hell, is that all you're worried about? Cab fare, I'll pay your cab fare." Said Bradley as he took his wallet out of his pants pocket. "How much do you need, twenty dollars?"

"No," said Jackie, "it's more than that."

"Forty dollars."

"I have to tip him, you want me to tip him don't you?"

"Eighty dollars for a cab, woman you're crazy."

Jackie was standing completely naked before him except for her white, lace panties. She was still fondling her perfect breasts, making the pink nipples stand as erect as Bradley's penis.

"Well, I guess I had just better take the bus home."

"Shit, here's a hundred dollars. Now get your ass in here and earn it."

Jackie put the money in her purse and slowly rolled her panties down to the top of her patchy black pubic hair. Bradley was still sitting on the edge of the bed going crazy. Jackie walked right up to him and shoved his face in her crotch.

Jackie's talcomed body carried a hint of perfumed fragrance. Bradley pulled her panties down and threw her on the bed. Bradley was a dog in heat. He had no sense of foreplay or sensitivity, he rolled over on top of her and forced himself in. Jackie, still turned on from the exotic dancer, her lubricated body accepted his small intrusion without consequence.

Bradley moaned and groaned and in just seconds fell from his elbows, which had been bracing his stocky body, to his full weight laying on her chest.

"What? That's it?" Jackie yelled at him as she pushed him off. "What about me? You're all through?"

"You got your money. Since when did a hooker ever care about fulfillment? I thought the quicker the better for you girls."

"Is that what you think, I'm a hooker?"

"You wanted money, you're a hooker, or do you prefer the term prostitute, or maybe slut, which one is it?" Bradley was caustic in his reply.

Jackie went into the bathroom with her clothes and started to cry. She heard what Bradley had said and it hurt. It hurt because Jackie knew he was telling the truth.

She got dressed quickly and went back out into the bedroom to find Bradley was already gone.

Jackie, coming down from her drug induced high, sat on the edge of the bed and cried. Hearing the sound of a key in the room door caused Jackie to stand up quickly and in a fright of sobriety expected Bradley had forgotten something and was returning for it.

It wasn't Bradley. It was no one she remembered meeting before, she was petrified with fright.

"Who are you? What do you want?" Jackie shouted at the tall man in a charcoal gray suit, as he entered the room walking in her direction.

"It doesn't matter who I am, does it? Just call me, John. That's the term you girls use for your tricks, isn't it?"

"What girls? What tricks are you talking about?" Jackie was screaming at the intruder.

"Bradley tells me you didn't get his money's worth,

I'm here to resolve that."

"Get out of my way," Jackie yelled, "I'm leaving."

"Not until I say so." He grabbed Jackie by her forearm and threw her to the bed.

Jackie tried to slap him with her free arm. He grabbed it and pinned both of her hands over her head to the bed while he sat on her waist.

"You're a spunky bitch aren't you."

"I'm not a bitch, get off of me." Jackie was crying and kicking, he was too big and heavy, she couldn't move.

Then using one hand to hold both of hers, he began unbuttoning her blouse. Once opened, he nuzzled his face between her breasts and kissed her. He kissed her cleavage and neck. The more he kissed her the less she struggled.

Still sitting on her he began to take off his shirt. He didn't speak, just undressed to his waist, then got up and removed his trousers. Jackie lay sobbing on the bed. Her visitor removed her clothing and forced himself into her.

Unlike Bradley, he was big and rough. Penetration hurt.

"No, no, you're hurting me," Jackie begged.

He didn't pay attention, instead he began to form a rhythmic pattern to his thrusts.

Jackie opened her legs wider to accommodate him and increase her enjoyment. His movement was singularly strong and defined. Jackie hooked his back with her legs and hugged his neck with her arms. She was receiving deep and burning penetration, but the more it hurt, the more sensuous it became.

Finally he began to move more quickly, and with a loud, "Aahh shit," he stiffened and as if harpooning a whale entered her with one last forceful thrust.

Their two bodies melded with sweat. Jackie, overcome with her first encounter with rough sex, sobbed quietly to herself. Her body was in favor of the ordeal, although her conscience objected vehemently. Finally she slid out from under him, quickly got dressed, again, and left the room.

Jackie's first thought was to go into the lounge, see if Bradley was there and scratch his eyes out. Maybe she would embarrass him in front of his friends. As mad as she was, reason won out. She knew better than to create a scene, besides, for reasons she couldn't explain, her body wanted to thank him.

Jackie made her way to the front door of the Towers and had the door-man hail her a cab. For just a fleeting second Jackie prayed the cab wouldn't be Joe's.

"I hope you enjoyed your evening with us," the door man said as he held the cab door open for Jackie.

"Yes, fine," was her only reply. Jackie got in and gave the driver her address.

The ride home gave Jackie time to reflect on the events of the evening.

To the best of her knowledge she had never done any kind of drugs, except for the ones the doctor had prescribed. Her encounter with Monica's brownies left her questioning her moralistic beliefs. The brownies were drug laden, but other than feeling terrifically relaxed and self- confident she couldn't find a valid argument against what had happened. "After all," she rationalized to herself, "if it hadn't been for the brownies, the prude that I am wouldn't have allowed me to enjoy the male dancer." And she certainly did enjoy the dancer.

"And what about Bradley?" She rationalized, "If it hadn't been for the brownies I wouldn't have led him on. It was at my suggestion that he go and get a room key, not his."

Jackie thought back to the vision of the poor man sitting naked on the bed wanting her so badly that he couldn't control himself. She smiled quietly remembering how worked up he became as she undressed slowly in front of him. She had discovered something new about herself she hadn't known before; the erotic act of disrobing was extremely stimulating for her also. Bradley would have paid her any amount to complete the sex act. She patted herself on the back for the novel way she had gotten Bradley to contribute to her financial gain.

Then her smile turned to bitter self-castigation. The old Jackie would have never gone to a bar to pick up a man; and to ask for money for sexual favors was surely the ultimate sin for a woman.

Jackie was trying to trade morals for ideals; excuse licentious behavior for the fear of failure and depravation.

Jackie tried to make herself feel guilty for the way she behaved, but in truth she enjoyed the new feeling of liberation. The old Jackie would have been quietly ashamed and withdrawn.

Then with a calm and newly defined sense of sexual achievement Jackie re-lived the second encounter with Bradley's friend; who threw her on the bed and had his way with her. She remembered the strength of his hands as he felt her body and the force of his sex as he penetrated her. She remembered the pleasure it had brought her. At the time of the act she was ashamed for enjoying what she would have otherwise considered an animalistic sexual encounter. She was more afraid than hurt. He had such control, he lasted much longer than Harry ever did; and poor Bradley, he didn't last at all.

Jackie was managing to rationalize her entire evening. As much as she knew she should be disgusted with herself, she felt strength with the mature way she had handled the confrontation. Also, she knew she needed the money she had earned, even with Joe's help she couldn't make it on her own. Jackie kept reassuring herself each time her morals began to make headway that this was only temporary.

"You're home, miss, that will be eighteen fifty."

Jackie handed him a twenty and told him to keep the change.

"Gee, are you sure you can afford it?" The cab driver was less than appreciative.

Jackie slammed the cab door and told him to get the hell out of her sight, then went to her apartment. She had enough for one evening. Jackie felt her world coming apart, her legs were weak, her stomach nauseous, and she didn't want to be on the street when it happened.

10   ONE GOOD DEED
LEADS TO ANOTHER

Joe looked at his watch: it was one-fifteen. The bars all closed at two am on Sunday mornings. They closed at three am on Saturday mornings. Some years back a religious group thought that if the bars closed earlier on Sunday morning more people would go to church. So in order not to lose too many votes the town council moved closing time back one hour.

Joe didn't like to pick up drinkers. Most of them were obnoxious, lousy tippers and prone to get sick in his cab. Tonight he had a call from the bartender of the Blue Moon Grotto to pick up a fare that had requested him.

Over the many years Joe had been driving a cab he had given out thousands and thousands of his business cards; every once in awhile someone would call.

The Blue Moon Grotto was what used to be an upscale disco. Disco had been out for years so the new owners upgraded the laser light show: nightly live D.J.'s and strippers in cages surrounded the upgraded dance floor. It was an older crowd, yuppies and middle aged-businessmen. The place had a good reputation, no fighting or drugs.

The night club had a long horseshoe driveway. Joe was in line behind a stretch limo. Eventually four women dressed to the nines followed by two men dressed in fancy suits got in and the limo drove off.

"I'm here on a call," Joe told the attendant.

"I'll go check." The red blazered doorman disappeared inside. He returned with a tall Latin looking man wearing a navy blue suit and a model-type arm-piece wearing almost nothing. Joe thought it was strange for a woman to almost freeze just to be in fashion.

The doorman held the door open for the couple then knocked on the roof signaling for Joe it was okay to leave.

"Good to see you again, my friend," the passenger said.

"I'm afraid you've got me at a disadvantage, I can't remember having you in my cab before," Joe said.

"It was almost two years ago. I was here on a business trip and left my wallet in your cab on a trip to the airport. Remember? You found it and had me paged so the security personnel could return it to me. I asked to thank you personally and was told you had a fare and couldn't wait. When I opened my wallet to check and see if anything was missing, I found your business card."

"Oh, yeah. Now I remember. I had a family that was in a hurry to go, so I gave my card to Airport Security and told them to call me if you didn't claim your wallet. I had forgotten all about it." Joe smiled after recalling the incident.

"Well, Joe, I was on my way to meet my fiancee that night, and if it hadn't been for your honesty my trip would have been a disaster. I am now a happily married man. This is my wife Erica."

"Pleased to meet you, Erica, I'm afraid you've got me at a disadvantage, I don't remember your name," Joe said.

"Ricardo, but please call me Ricky."
Joe and his two fares had a brief but pleasant conversation on the way back to Ricky's hotel.

"Joe, my plane leaves at two tomorrow afternoon, would you please pick us up?"

"Sure, you bet."

The cab pulled in front of the hotel and Ricky and Erica got out. Ricky took a bill out of his pocket, folded it up and handed it to Joe.

"Keep the change, and thanks again."

Joe didn't look at the bill. He never did in front of a customer, he felt it was rude. He placed the rolled up bill in his shirt pocket for the time being.

"See you tomorrow at noon."

The noon was on Sunday. Even though Joe didn't work on Sundays there were times he made exceptions.

Seeing someone he had helped years before who took the time out to thank him gave Joe a warm feeling inside. Even though Joe had helped many strangers over the years very few ever took time to thank him. Joe decided to take one last swing by the bus station since he was already on that side of town.

There were at least ten cabs in line and no activity. It looked like he was done for the evening. Joe turned his sign to 'Off Duty.' He decided to drive by Green's Deli and get his nightly cup of coffee before going home.

The light on the corner near the bus station turned red so Joe stopped. He looked around and noticed he was the only car at the intersection. It was times like this when he was tempted to run the light. Joe hadn't had a moving violation since long before Martha died and he didn't care to start now.

The light turned green and Joe made a left turn onto fourteenth street. As he did there was a young girl with long blond hair hitch-hiking. It was very late, and very cold. All she was wearing was a windbreaker. Joe pulled over. The girl came over to the cab, opened the passenger door and asked, "Are you off duty, because I don't have any money."

"I'm on my way home, but I'll give you a lift. Get in."

While Joe was distracted, talking to the girl, a young man dressed in dark clothes yanked Joe's door open and yelled, "Get out of the cab or I'll shoot."

Joe turned to see who belonged to the voice; all he could see when he turned around was the barrel of a pistol pointed at his nose. The young man was waving it in his face and screaming for him to get out or he would shoot. Joe wasn't one to be foolish or brave so he got out.

"What do you want?" Joe said as he faced the boy.

"Turn around and put your hands on the roof." Joe did as he was told.

"Tina, come get his money."

The girl ran around the cab and took Joe's wallet out of his pocket. He had a good night and there was over two hundred dollars in it.

"Please take the money but leave me my papers," Joe pleaded.

"Shut up!" the youth shouted. "How much did we get?" he asked Tina.

"I don't know," Tina said gleefully, "but he's loaded. Come on, let's go."

"Please, just leave me my..."

Joe never got to finish, the youth with the gun hit Joe on the back of his head and knocked him out.

When he woke up the ambulance attendants were loading him onto a gurney into the back of an ambulance. One of the attendants was shining a small flashlight into his eyes checking for dilation.

"What happened? How did you get here?" Joe asked the attendant.

"Can I talk to him?" a policeman asked.

"Yeah, sure. I think he'll be okay but we're going to take him in overnight for observation."

A uniformed policeman climbed in the back of the ambulance and sat next to Joe.

"Did you see who did this?"

"Where's my cab? Where's my wallet? Did they take my wallet?" Joe had more questions than the officer did.

"Calm down, Mr. Williams, one of your fellow cab drivers saw them hit you and called it in on his radio. They threw your wallet down on the street as they ran away. Now, did you know them?"

Joe explained the sequence of events leading to the robbery and gave the police the best description he could.

The officer took detailed notes and when he was done told Joe someone would be contacting him soon to arrange a time when a police sketch artist could come by and make a composite drawing.

"What about my cab?" Joe asked.

"We contacted your company. They said they would send someone over to take it to the compound until you're better. Is there anyone you would like us to contact?"

Joe thought about Jackie. He decided he didn't know her well enough to bother her at this late hour and told the officer no. After all he would be going home first thing in the morning; which was only hours away.

It was the first time Joe had ever ridden in an ambulance. The siren was sounding and the lights flashing; Joe found it exciting. At the hospital the emergency room was noisy with a lot of activity around Joe. Finally, the hustle and bustle ceased and the emergency room doctor came by to check him.

"Good evening, Mr. Williams, how are you feeling?"

"I'm feeling fine, Doc, when can I go home?"

"It all depends on your X-rays. You took a nasty blow to the head, and we want to keep you in here long enough to make sure you don't have a concussion."

"How long will that be?" Joe asked.

"If all of your signs are negative and your pictures okay, I would think by tomorrow evening."

"Tomorrow evening, I can't be here till then. Who will take care of Felix?" Joe was noticeably upset.

"Who's Felix?" the doctor asked trying to calm him down.

"My cat--he's never been left alone."

"Well now, we can't have that, can we." The doctor saw how upset Joe was getting and decided to make a change.

"Who do you know that can run by and check in on him, and I'll see what I can do about getting you released a little earlier?"

The phone rang at four in the morning. Jackie thought she was having a bad dream and it would go away. Sitting straight up in bed she realized it wasn't a dream.

A weak hello was all she could muster.

"Jackie Jones please." Came a clinical sounding voice over the phone.

"This is me, I mean I'm her. Who's calling?"

"This is Doctor Johnson from County General. Now don't get upset, but Joe Williams has been in an accident."

The doctor went into great detail explaining the events of the evening and assuring her that there wasn't a life threatening situation. He went on to explain Joe's concern about his cat Felix and asked if she would look in on him. It would help Joe to rest easier. Jackie assured the doctor she would and asked him to tell Joe not to worry.

* * * * *

The next morning Joe woke up in his hospital bed, and for just a second had forgotten where he was. He tried to sit up too quickly and fell back against his pillow in pain.

"Ooh, my head."

Joe felt someone holding his hand. "Joe, are you all right? Where does it hurt?" came a soft caring voice.

Joe opened his eyes and turned his head towards the soft voice.

"Jackie, what are you doing here? Where is Felix?"

"Felix is fine. I left him about two hours ago and came right over here, I thought you might need me."

Jackie was holding Joe's hand in both of hers. She looked at Joe's face, it was a swollen mess. When the robber hit him on the head he fell face first onto the street, bloodied his nose and gave himself a black eye. Truly he looked much worse than he was.

"How did you get here?" Joe wanted to know.

"I called the cab company you work for, Joe, and they picked me up and brought me right over. They didn't charge me either, and the dispatcher asked me to tell you your cab was in good condition, and you shouldn't worry."

"Well that is good news," Joe paused. "Now tell me about Felix, is he all right?"

"I went right over to your house early this morning when the hospital woke me up. Felix met me at the side door, just like he did when I came over for dinner. He has plenty of food and water, and I even changed his litter box. I was so tired I sat down in your chair for just a minute and fell fast asleep. And you know what Joe, when I woke up Felix was asleep on my lap."

"Oh my God, what time is it?" Joe almost yelled.

"Just after eleven, why?" Jackie answered, upset with Joe's change in temperament.

"Give me the phone, quick, I've got a special customer to pick up at noon., He's counting on me to take him to the airport on time."

Jackie dialed the phone number Joe had given her and handed him the receiver, he explained the situation to dispatch and they said they would give his fare the red carpet treatment and explain why Joe wasn't there personally.

"That reminds me, Jackie, see if my clothes are in the closet there."

Jackie got up and went to the closet, "Yes, Joe, they are. Why?"

"See if there is some money in the shirt pocket. I usually put all my money in my wallet, but last night when I took my fare and his wife back to their hotel I put his tip in my pocket and never did look at it to see what it was."

Jackie fumbled around for a few seconds, "Yes, Joe there's something in this pocket. She reached in and pulled out a tightly rolled bill. When she unrolled it there were two one hundred dollar bills.

"Wow! Joe, this is some tip you got here." She handed Joe the money, "How did you rate such a large tip?"

"I returned his wallet a few years back with over five hundred dollars in it. I guess this is his way of saying thanks. It's a good thing too, that just about covers what the kids stole last night."

Jackie sat with Joe the rest of the afternoon and watched TV while Joe slept. It was about five when the doctor came in on his evening rounds. Joe was still asleep.

"How is he doing?" the doctor asked Jackie.

"He's been sleeping a lot, I guess that's good."

"Well it could be, and it could point to other problems. I'm going to order some more tests tomorrow morning."

"When can he go home, doctor?"

"I understand Mr. Williams lives alone. Is that right?"

"Yes."

"Well for starters he shouldn't drive for at least a week. And if he should fall at home he could do serious damage to himself before someone finds him. I think it best that he stays here for at least two or three more days where we can have a twenty-four hour watch over him."

"Oh, my!" said Jackie, "He'll never sit still for that." Then she paused pointedly before continuing, "What if I stay with him for a few days, will you let him go home then?"

"I'll tell you what," the doctor said, "let me see what the test results are tomorrow morning, and if everything is in the normal range he can go home only if he's under your care."

"What? Are you talking about me? What do you mean I can't go home? I'm leaving now!" Joe had awoken and came in on the end of the conversation. He made a feeble attempt to get up. As soon as he sat straight up, the pain returned in his head and he fell back on his pillow.

Jackie thanked the doctor and told him she would explain their conversation to Joe.

Just after the doctor left, a nurse brought in Joe's dinner. Jackie helped him eat and rehashed her conversation with the doctor to put Joe's mind at ease.

Joe was being stubborn. He had been taking care of himself and Felix for ten years now, and wasn't going to change.

"Joe," said Jackie quietly, "did you have to fix my shoe and bring it back to me?"

"Well, no," Joe muttered, "but I like doing things for people. It's my nature, besides it makes me feel good."

"Joe, I like doing things for people too, when I can. Don't you want me to feel good about helping someone?"

Joe didn't answer, he just pouted.

"I have some personal days off coming to me at work. I don't ever call in sick, and I've earned them. I'm going to call Dr. Jefferies tonight and tell him what happened and where I am. That way if there is an emergency he can reach me. That is unless you're going to deny me the opportunity to do a good deed."

Joe still didn't speak. He was having a hard time trying to find a good argument. Besides, he knew that if he wanted to go home it would have to be under someone's supervision or he would be staying in the hospital. Joe didn't even want to think about that.

He finally broke the silence, "I don't think the bed in the guest room has any sheet on it."

Jackie broke out in a big smile. She had developed a genuine fondness for Joe during their brief times together. Joe was a good person, and easy to like.

Jackie told Joe, "I'm going to have the cab company pick me up and take me to my apartment so I can pick up some personal things and then bring me back to the hospital."

Joe vetoed the idea. He said, "I don't need a nurse maid, I would rather have you spend the night with Felix. He's more afraid of being left alone than I am."

Jackie waited till after nine when Joe went to sleep like a log. Jackie was feeling the effects of her long day and knew she was running on fumes. She gave the night duty nurse Joe's home number and said to call her if she was needed. Jackie said she would try to be in early the next morning.

11   A TIME TO SOW

At seven o'clock the next morning the sounds of rattling dishes on the breakfast cart woke Joe up. He stared at the ceiling for a few minutes while he focused his eyes.

"Good morning, Mr. Williams," the nurse said while adjusting his bedside tray. "Did you have a good night's sleep?"

"Yes I did, as a matter of fact."

The nurse adjusted his bed to a more up-right position.

"How long has she been here?" Joe asked pointing to Jackie sleeping in a near-by chair.

"She came in about an hour ago, saying she was here to take you home if the doctor releases you. She must be a very special friend. You're a lucky man to have someone that nice to be worried about your well being."

Joe looked at the sleeping beauty, "Yes, I really am."

The nurse explained the morning itinerary. "As soon as breakfast is over you'll get your sponge bath and then it's down to X-ray for some pictures. And if you smile pretty the doctor may let you go home early."

"Sponge bath," Joe grumbled, "I don't need a sponge bath, I can wash myself when I get home."

"I'm sorry, Mr. Williams, but that's hospital policy."

"Ooh, my, I must have fallen asleep," Jackie said as she woke up, stretching and yawning.

"I don't care about policy. You're not giving me a sponge bath." Joe grumbled at the nurse.

"Well then, you can just stay here till you do. We're not going to send you home dirty. If you prefer, your friend can do it instead of me, but you're going to be clean."

Jackie's face turned bright red. She hoped beyond hopes that no one noticed.

"Fine!" Joe yelled at the nurse.

"Fine!" the nurse yelled back and pushed the cart out of the room.

Joe grumbled to himself as he ate his oatmeal and drank his orange juice.

Jackie, feeling a shortness of breath, quickly changed the subject.

"Look, Joe, Felix sent you a get well card." Jackie had taken a piece of stationary and written "Get well soon, I miss you-Love Felix". Then she put some of her lip-stick on one of his paws and signed the note with a paw print.

Her thoughtfulness touched Joe. It was the kind of thing Martha used to do for him. Joe was used to being kind and thoughtful of others, he wasn't used to receiving kindness, and felt awkward.

About a half hour went by and the morning nurse returned to pick up the dishes and drop off the small gray tub of disinfected water and a large sponge. "Now you be a good boy and wash behind your ears and maybe the doctor will give you a sucker," the nurse said with a chuckle.

Harry liked it when Martha used to wash his back, but everything else he washed himself.

Joe sat up on the bed and Jackie sat next to him. Joe's hospital gown opened from the back so she slid it off his shoulders and scrubbed his back with one hand while massaging his shoulder with the other.

"Ooh, that feels great. Martha used to give the best back rubs."

Jackie took the hint and put the sponge down and massaged his whole back. "I imagine you must be stiff laying here in one position," she said.

"Let's get this over with," Joe said and pressed the button on his control allowing the bed to lay flat. Then he lay on his stomach.

Jackie looked down at Joe's white skin. He still had some tan on his neck and fore-arms but other than that he was white. Joe was in good condition for his age, even though Jackie didn't know how old Joe was. She started washing his feet but stopped when Joe jumped.

"Did I hurt you?" Jackie gasped.

"No, not at all, it's just that my feet are ticklish."

Jackie picked up his foot and kissed it gently, "I'm sorry," she said "I'll be more careful."

Now it was Joe's turn to blush, never in all the time they were married did Martha kiss one of his feet.

Jackie carefully washed each leg stopping just below his buttocks. Then she decided to quickly pat it with the sponge.

Holding her breath she said, "Roll over."

Joe did as he was told, he rolled over on his back and looked directly at the ceiling so he wouldn't have to look at Jackie.

Since Jackie had already washed both of Joe's legs she folded his hospital garment down to just below his belly button covering his private parts and vigorously washed his chest. Joe didn't have much hair, just a small patch in the middle. Harry didn't have any hair at all. Jackie didn't know any better, she didn't care. Jackie washed everything down to Joe's belly button.

"Here," she said handing Joe the sponge, "you're on your own for the rest."

Both of them gave a sigh of relief.

An orderly came in with a wheelchair and took Joe down to X-ray.

Joe was gone for over an hour.

It was Monday morning, normally a work day for Jackie, but she had called Dr. Jefferies the night before and explained the situation. She had asked for three days' sick leave. Dr. Jefferies told her to take as much time as she needed.

Jackie was a good woman going through a mid-life crisis of sorts. Helping Joe was therapy for herself as well. Jackie sat alone, smiling to herself, thinking about how she and Joe got to become friends.

"The doctor will be in around lunch time," the orderly said while wheeling Joe back into the room. "He'll have had time to read your pictures by then.

"Yeah, thanks," Joe grunted.

The orderly helped Joe back into his bed. Joe was noticeably tired. It concerned Jackie.

Jackie watched game shows on TV while Joe slept. Jackie hadn't watched daytime TV since Harry had left. After an hour of it she knew she wasn't missing anything.

The doctor came in just after lunch. Joe and Jackie were laying in ambush.

"Look, Mr. Williams," the doctor said in a pointedly serious manner, "there are still some concerns here, but on the condition you're not going to be left alone I'm going to let you go home." Then turning to Jackie, "I expect you to let me know immediately if he experiences dizziness or memory loss."

"Yes sir, doctor," was all Jackie had to say.

"Good, then I'll see you again in one week, and if you're okay I'll give you permission to drive. Until then, no driving, am I understood?"

"But, but...," Joe tried to speak.

"You have my word on it," Jackie interrupted.

Joe's cab company came to the hospital and picked up Joe and Jackie in Joe's own taxicab. There was another cab following behind so they could leave Joe his cab and the other driver would have a ride back to the station.

"Do you know how to drive?" Joe asked Jackie.

"Yes, Joe, just because I ride a bus doesn't mean I don't know how to drive," said Jackie with an attitude of indignation.

Jackie put Joe in the passenger seat and pulled out of the hospital parking lot. "Should I turn on the meter?" Jackie laughed at the thought of charging Joe to ride in his own cab.

Joe was a terrible passenger. He kept giving directions and pointing out cars that were changing lanes without signaling. Finally Jackie pulled the cab into Joe's driveway; there in the window was Felix.

Joe was so filled with emotion that he didn't wait for Jackie to open his door, instead he left her behind and went straight for the kitchen door and to an awaiting friend.

"Felix, did you miss me? I hope you're not mad." Felix purred so loud the dishes rattled and Joe hugged his furry friend. Then just as they had been doing for years, Joe and Felix went into the living room, sat down in Joe's recliner and watched TV.

Jackie was touched by the emotional reunion between the two friends. She went to Joe's bedroom and turned down the sheets. She found some old slippers in his closet and returned with them to the living room. Without asking, Jackie took Joe's shoes off and replaced them with the slippers.

Joe didn't know quite what to say. He was both honored and embarrassed. "Gee, Jackie, you didn't have to do that."

"Does that mean I can't?" Jackie snapped back. Her face as well as her voice reflected her feelings on the subject.

Her reaction took Joe by surprise, "Well, no, of course not. I just meant..."

"Since you didn't ask me to do it, perhaps it's something I want to do." Jackie was matter-of-fact with her reply. Joe decided to drop the subject.

"I need to go and pick up a few things for the house. Promise not to leave the chair until I get back from the store."

"I'll promise on one condition." Joe reached into his shirt pocket and handed Jackie one of the hundred dollar bills. "You take this and buy whatever you think this house needs."

"Keep your money Joe, I'm not broke." Jackie was trying to show her independence.

"Then I'll not promise."

Jackie really didn't have any extra money so she took Joe's and smiled.

"Is there anything you know of that you need?" she asked.

"Sunday is my day for running errands, so why don't you look around the house and buy whatever you think needs buying."

Jackie wandered around the house with a note pad looking into the cabinets, the refrigerator, and even the medicine cabinet. Wherever she went, Felix followed.

Jackie returned with a bathrobe she had taken from Joe's closet.

"Before I leave, I want you to get out of those nasty clothes. Here put this on. And one more thing, promise me you won't try and take a shower unless I'm in the house."

"I promise," came a weak reply.

"You're not very convincing, but I trust you to keep your word. When I get back I'm going to do laundry and I expect those clothes you're wearing to be in the hamper." Jackie's voice carried a certain quality of authoritarianism.

Jackie left Joe and Felix watching TV while she drove Joe's cab over to the shopping center to fill her list. As Jackie pushed her cart through the grocery laden isles she realized a feeling of completeness she hadn't know for a long time, a feeling of being needed, being useful and appreciated. Jackie smiled and walked a little taller.

She had forgotten to bring her tooth brush so she bought a new one, and her favorite tooth paste; just a small tube. Jackie never kept food in her apartment, mostly because she couldn't afford it, and found she enjoyed shopping for groceries again. She bought several large bottles of the same kind of soda Joe had bought on her first visit, and then she passed the pretzels. Actually she didn't pass the pretzels, Jackie hadn't bought herself a bag of pretzels in almost a year. The big log rolls with lots of salt. She hesitated for a few seconds, dealing with the guilt of buying something Harry used to call frivolous with someone else's money. "I'll pay for them out of my own pocket," she thought and threw them in the cart.

After getting paper towels, napkins, toilet paper, some fresh vegetables, chicken, fish and a bunch of fresh cut flowers for the table, Jackie was ready to go home.

While standing in the check-out line Jackie read the magazine covers. A book of cross-word puzzles caught her eye. Jackie had been a cross-word junkie at one time until Harry had convinced her it was a waste of time.

Jackie paid the bill and took the few bags of groceries to the cab. It had been a while since Jackie had driven a car. She enjoyed the freedom it allowed.

When she got back to Joe's, Jackie carried all the bags into the kitchen. Then she walked quietly towards the sound of the TV in the living room. Joe was sound asleep in his recliner with Felix asleep on his lap. Joe was wearing the bath robe. Jackie smiled with self-content.

Jackie put the groceries away and started cooking dinner. The rattling of pots and pans awoke Felix, and aroused his curiosity.

"Hello, Felix, did you come to help?"

Felix crawled into a brown paper grocery bag that was laying sideways on the kitchen floor and hid.

Jackie went to the bathroom and retrieved all the dirty clothes from the hamper. Joe had left his uniform on top. She went to the utility room and started a load. Then she trimmed the bunch of flowers, placed them in a vase and carried them to the dining room table.

"Is that you, Jackie?" Joe's voice called from the next room.

"Yes, Joe," she answered and went in to see how he was doing.

"Did you get everything you needed?"

" Everything and a few extras."

"What kind of extras? I'm not sure I follow you."

"Just a second and I'll show you." With that Jackie disappeared to the kitchen and returned seconds later with a brown bag.

Joe adjusted his chair to the upright position so he could see better. Felix took sentry on his lap.

"Let's see what we've got here? Aha!" Jackie put her hand in the bag. Then she briskly shook her hand back and forth, creating a jingling sound. Felix began to meow loudly with anticipation.

"Look, Felix, a furry cotton mouse with a bell." Jackie threw the toy across the room and Felix took off after it like a bat out of hell. Joe and Jackie both laughed.

"Joe," Jackie said in a more serious tone, "I notice you don't smoke, but while I was going to the store I saw your ashtray was filled with candy wrappers. Tootsie Rolls to be precise, so if you're a good boy these are for you." Jackie held up a one pound bag of the candy.

"Aw, Jackie, that's awfully nice of you. Martha used to buy the big bags like that, put some in a small candy dish and then hide the rest of them so I wouldn't eat them all at once...," Joe's voice began to crack, "come here..., please."

Jackie walked over to Joe and he gave her a bear hug around her waist. Jackie in turn hugged Joe's neck. The two stood quietly enjoying the brief moment of tranquility, then Felix jumped up carrying his new toy.

After dinner Jackie agreed to let Joe take a shower with the condition that he leave the bathroom door open. That way if he should fall or need help Jackie would hear him. Joe made Jackie promise not to peek.

Joe disappeared and proceeded to shower while Jackie and Felix cleared the dinner dishes.

"Gosh, Jackie, I can't begin to tell you how much better I feel now that I'm clean all over... and under." Joe laughed.

With the dinner dishes washed and put away Jackie took advantage of the quiet to get her shower in. Since she didn't have one in her apartment, it was great to wash her hair in a shower for a change.

When she got out of the bath wearing only a large towel wrapped around her small frame she saw that Joe had found Martha's old bath robe and placed it on her bed for her, Jackie was deeply touched.

The rest of the evening Joe watched TV with Felix asleep on his lap while Jackie sat on the sofa next to Joe and did crossword puzzles.

Few words were spoken. The stress-free atmosphere of the room provided each with an inner calm neither had enjoyed for a long time. It was the kind of feeling that you don't recognize as having lost until you find it again.

When the late news came on Joe got up to turn off the TV and saw that Jackie was asleep on the couch. His first impulse was to gently shake her awake, instead he just stood over her for a brief moment and smiled at his sleeping beauty. Then he went to the guest room and returned with a blanket, placed it over her and turned off the lamp. Joe left the kitchen light on in case Jackie got up in the middle of the night and couldn't see. Joe smiled and said "Good night, Jackie. And thanks," as he walked by.

12   ANOTHER DAY WITH JOE

The next morning, Tuesday, Jackie woke up on the couch to the sound of a purring Felix sleeping on her hip. Jackie lay there for many minutes looking out the Bay window at the rising sun. She was enjoying a warm fuzzy feeling of inner peace she hadn't known since she couldn't remember when. She pulled the blanket Joe had placed over her under her chin and smiled inside, appreciating the caring gesture.

Where Jackie lived all she could see was the alley, that is when she lifted her shades, which was almost never; she was afraid of being shot.

The leaves had turned colors for one more season, the only leaves left were brown and stubborn. A squirrel landed on the window ledge and chattered argumentatively as he peered in the window. Felix, protecting Jackie's privacy, ran to the window sill and chased him away.

"Good boy, Felix," Jackie called out, "you show him who's boss." Jackie hugged the sofa pillow and smiled from ear to ear. She felt secure and happy.

She looked at her watch: it was seven-ten. It wasn't like her to sleep in. Every day she always woke up before the alarm went off on work days. Jackie passed it off as stress and exhaustion. Then the smell of fresh brewing coffee found its way to her delicate nostrils.

Before Jackie could get up, Joe appeared with a TV tray and two cups of coffee. "Cream and sugar, right?"

"Right." Jackie sat up and tied her terry-cloth robe snugly around her waist. "Joe, I'm supposed to be taking care of you, not the other way around." "So! The doctor didn't say I couldn't make a pot of coffee, now did he?"

Joe sat the tray in front of Jackie, took his cup over to his recliner, pointed the remote at the TV and switched on the "Today" program. "When I get to be a hundred I hope Willard is still doing the weather so he'll announce my birthday on TV."

"You've got a long way to go before that happens, Joe," Jackie said.

"Not really, Jackie, I'm going to be fifty-five this year."

"Well, Joe, you don't look a day over forty." Jackie said with a smile. "And thanks for covering me up last night, I didn't mean to fall asleep on you."

Jackie had bought some fruit, she had that for breakfast, Joe had two more cups of coffee.

The rest of the day Jackie spent house cleaning. She took down all the curtains, took the covers off the furniture, scrubbed walls and kept very busy. Joe and

Felix watched TV and the two of them catnapped all afternoon long.

Jackie was dusting the low-boy next to the china hutch when something caught her eye. There on the second shelf was a collection of music boxes. Jackie loved music boxes and couldn't resist opening the hutch and holding them one at a time. They were porcelain, and crystal, and one was hand carved wooden with a beautiful oak leaf on top. Jackie twisted the key and put it down on the counter. With crystal clarity it began to play a familiar tune; Mac Arthur Park. Tears came to her eyes as she rewound the magic box and listened to the tune for a second time before putting it back on the shelf in it's place. Jackie found solace and personal satisfaction knowing she shared something special with Joe's Martha.

While Joe was on his third nap of the day Jackie started a meatloaf. She chopped up lots of celery and onions and used bread crumbs as an extender. She was folding the laundry in the utility room when Joe woke up.

"Gosh, Jackie, something sure smells good. What is it?"

"Dinner."

"Well, I know that. What is it we are having for dinner?"

"You'll find out at dinner, now go sit down."

"Look, Jackie, I didn't expect you to be doing all this house cleaning and such. Please slow down, I'm beginning to feel guilty."

"Nonsense. If you want to help go set the table."
Joe smiled, "Martha used to have me set the table."

Jackie had meatloaf that she shaped in the form of a taxi. It didn't really look like a taxi, but it did sort of resemble a car. Jackie also made a special meat loaf meat ball just for Felix.

After dinner, Joe, over Jackie's objections, helped with the dishes. Then the two of them retired to the living room. Joe and Felix watched TV and Jackie did cross-word puzzles; just like an old married couple.

"Joe, I'm going to take my shower now, if you don't mind."

"For goodness sakes, Jackie, please do."

Jackie left Joe stroking Felix.

"You know, Felix, we are two very lucky guys to have such a nice person help us like this."

It wasn't long before Jackie reappeared in Martha's old, freshly washed, robe with her hair in a towel. "The bathroom is all yours, Joe, any time you want."

Jackie went back to her puzzles and Joe headed off to the shower. Jackie was trying to figure out eighteen across, it started with 'd' a word for..., when she heard a crash, and a yell from the bathroom. Jackie jumped up and ran yelling, "Joe, Joe, are you all right?"

Joe was on the bottom of the tub with the shower curtain on top of him with the water spraying and splashing all over the place.

Jackie was too upset to notice Joe's birthday suit.

"Joe, Joe, are you all right?"

At first Joe didn't say anything, he just thrashed around in the tub trying to get the wet shower curtain off his head and neck. Jackie reached down to untangle them still calling out his name, getting herself soaked while doing so.

Finally she managed to pull the curtain out of the tub all together and reached in over Joe to turn off the water.

"Joe, are you all right? What happened?"

Joe pulled himself up to a standing position. He looked frightened and embarrassed, "I stepped on the bar of soap and fell. Instinctively I grabbed for the first thing I could and it was the shower curtain."

All of a sudden it occurred to both of them that Joe was naked. Jackie turned a red face away and Joe tried to cover himself with the wash cloth. Jackie took the towel off her head and without turning around handed it to Joe, then left the room.

It only took Joe a few quick minutes to dry off and return to the living room and Jackie. Joe was embarrassed and Jackie was relieved. The two of them had a good laugh.

The next day Jackie called Joe's doctor to give him an update on Joe's condition. The doctor didn't like the fact that Joe was sleeping a lot; Jackie didn't mention the shower curtain incident. The doctor made an appointment for Joe to come in for a follow up visit Friday of the same week. He also told Jackie there wasn't any reason for her to stay any longer, that Joe should be just fine.

"Joe, I've got good news, the doctor said you're doing so well he's canceling your nursing service. He does want you to come in Friday morning at ten just to make sure it's okay for you to drive your cab again." Jackie was trying to keep a positive expression on her face; a tear in her eye reflected her true feelings. She turned and walked quickly to her room.

Joe sat in his recliner petting Felix trying to absorb the information he had just received. The full impact was being repelled by denial. Jackie would be going home, to her home. He wanted to say, "Gee, Jackie, that's great news, you'll get to go home." He knew that may sound to her that he wanted to get rid of her. He thought of saying, "I'm sure you'll be glad to be going back to work," but somehow that sounded like she would be happy to be leaving. Joe didn't know what to say or how to handle the situation. He picked up Felix and went to Jackie's room and knocked on her door.

"Jackie, can I talk to you for a moment, please?"

Jackie opened the door, it was evident from her red eyes that she had been crying.

"I know you're going to have to return to your own life, and, well...," Joe was having trouble getting his words out, "I would like to take you out to dinner on your last night here. I guess I should pick you up around six." Joe didn't wait for a reply, he turned and went back to his recliner. Jackie shut her bedroom door.

"Pick you up about six" I said, "How stupid can you be, Joe, you dumb-ass you." Joe was cursing himself out, "She lives here, you can't pick her up."

Joe sat quietly with the TV off and fell asleep.

Later that afternoon Jackie was in the kitchen preparing sandwiches for lunch. She was getting hungry and knew she couldn't hold out till dinner. Joe came up from behind her and started to put his hands on her shoulders, hesitated, then didn't.

Jackie felt his presence and waited for him to touch her. She held her breath, her shoulders tensed with anticipation. When he did not she was upset.

Joe put both hands in his pockets, resisting an urge to hug her. He could feel his voice begin to break before he spoke his first words.

"I hope you like Italian? There is this neighborhood restaurant near the cleaners that has the best home-made garlic bread sticks."

"I love Italian," Jackie said as she turned to face Joe and handed him a plate with two sandwiches.

"Look, Jackie, before, when I, well...," Joe took the plate and said, "thanks."

Jackie felt the same frustration. She had things she wanted to say to Joe, but she didn't know what, or even where to start.

Jackie read until five that day then disappeared into her room to get dressed. Joe went into his room and did the same. When Joe emerged twenty minutes later he was wearing a Navy-blue sport coat over charcoal gray slacks. He even had his hair combed.

"No, Felix, I can't pick you up, you'll get me dirty." Jackie came out of her room wearing a cranberry blazer over a white blouse, designer jeans, and the high heel shoes Joe had fixed for her.

"Wow!" said Joe. "You look good enough to take out and sit by the window."

He held his arm out for her, she took it with a smile, and they left for the cab.

"I guess you're still driving," Joe said.

"I guess so."

"Well, I can still be a gentleman," and with that Joe held the car door open for Jackie.

The drive to the restaurant was short. Joe pointed out the turns and reminded her to watch for the cars in front of them.

Because it was a weeknight the small restaurant wasn't crowded. They had their choice of seats. All the tables had red and white checkered tablecloths with an empty Chianti bottle and a candle on top in the center.

It was a cozy restaurant. There was a mural of Italy along one long wall, and Italian music was playing in the back ground.

Joe held Jackie's chair while she sat down, she acknowledged with a smile.

"Order anything you like," Joe boasted,as he sat down across from her.

The waiter brought a basket of garlic bread sticks to the table and asked, "Would you like something to drink?"
Joe didn't think to ask Jackie if she had a preference, "Something red in a bottle."

"Something red in a bottle," Jackie mocked him.

"Well, yeah, I don't know all those Italian names, I just know with Italian food you're suppose to order red wine."

Jackie smiled, she knew Joe was trying to impress her, but he didn't have to, she was already impressed.
For dinner Jackie let Joe order.

"Cappellini Florentine, and Caesar salad," Joe told the waiter.

When the waiter brought the wine, he uncorked it and poured a small glass for Joe to test. Joe drank it straight down and said, "That's great, fill'er up."
It was a quiet dinner. Occasionally Joe would think of a funny story about some fare he had picked up over the years and told it. Martha knew them by heart but Jackie was a fresh audience and laughed when she was supposed to. Joe only had two glasses

of wine, Jackie had the rest. By the end of the evening she was glassy-eyed and quite relaxed.

Joe declined dessert. He sat back in his chair and patted his stomach.

"Jackie, the food here is almost as good as what you make."

Jackie smiled and looked somewhat embarrassed.

"I'm going to miss you, Jackie. Running into you was a Godsend. I never said that to another woman except Martha. I, uh, just wanted you to know that."

Jackie got up, went over to Joe and kissed him square on his lips. "Joe, I'm going to miss you too, but I'm still your maid, remember. I get to come by twice a month and help out, I'll see you then."

"That reminds me, this is for you," Joe reached in his pocket and handed Jackie the other hundred dollar bill he had received as a tip.

"I can't take your money."

"Look, Jackie, you have more than earned it. If I had had to hire a private duty nurse it would have cost me much more, and I wouldn't have gotten my house cleaned in the process. Now, please, for me, take it."

Jackie wanted to put on airs, but she knew how badly she needed the money so she took it.

She tried to thank him, but she couldn't speak. Her eyes welled up with tears, and Joe, seeing Jackie, followed suit.

"Let's go down the street, I have one more thing I want to show you before we go home."

The two got back in the cab and Joe directed her to a spot in the shopping center near the end.

"Pull up there." Joe pointed out an empty parking space. It was an ice cream store.

"Come on, Jackie, when is the last time you had a banana-split?"

Jackie giggled with enthusiasm. "Honestly, Joe, I don't know if I've ever had one."

Joe ordered two super splits. Each of them got to pick out the kinds of ice cream and toppings they wanted. Joe had some of everything. Jackie had vanilla with the standard flavors of syrup.

It was like a first date. Joe dribbled chocolate syrup down his chin and Jackie wiped it clean with her napkin. Joe gave Jackie his cherries because he said they were fattening.

The ride home was like attending a funeral; it was deathly quiet in the cab. Neither knew what to say or how to express their innermost feelings. A strange thing happened when Jackie pulled the cab in the driveway; Joe reached over and gave Jackie's hand a squeeze. Joe's warm and affectionate touch took her by surprise.

Not knowing how to respond she said, "Look, Joe, our baby sitter is waiting up for us," pointing to Felix. Jackie spent the next day preparing meals and wrapping them in foil or saran wrap. She made TV dinners for Joe and put them in his freezer. The house was spotless and had a cheery, lived-in warmth that only comes with a happy home.

Joe had called his cab company to come pick up Jackie and take her home. She had a lot to do before going to work the next day. Jackie made Joe reserve a cab ride to the doctor the next day; he still wasn't cleared to drive.

The closer it came to the time for Jackie to leave, the fewer words were spoken. Voices were failing and tears were being forced back.

Finally the honking cab from the street established the urgency of reality.

Joe picked up Jackie's bag and carried it out to the cab for her. Joe was a gentleman and Jackie liked the feeling of being treated like a lady. Joe held the door open for her and she reached around Joe's waist and gave him a big bear hug. Joe held her tightly. Fearing to speak, he shut the door and waved to her as the cab backed down the driveway.

Joe returned to the house and made one quick phone call. Joe was an emotional man, a sensitive man. It made him feel good inside when he was able to do special things for someone else. Especially if that someone was a person he cared about. Joe cared about Jackie.

"Hello, florist, do you deliver? Yes, well I need a delivery made tonight. I don't care if it does cost extra, I want a dozen yellow gladiolas delivered tonight. Yes, I want the card to read, 'I miss you already. Thanks for everything,' and sign it Felix."

13 GIRLS NIGHT OUT

Jackie had only been home for thirty minutes when the door-bell rang. After asking "Who's there?" Jackie couldn't get her apartment door open fast enough.

"Are you Jackie Jones?" asked the uniformed courrier.

"Yes I am," reported Jackie gleefully.

"Delivery, sign here." The florist handed Jackie a long green box with a yellow ribbon tied around it. Quickly she shut and locked the door behind her and carried her package to the kitchen table to read the card; she smiled and thought of the card she gave Joe. Carefully she removed the bow and opened the box. The flowers were beautiful. Gladiolas were one of her favorites.

Her first thought was to call Joe and thank him, but she decided against it. Instead she would wait until after his doctor visit. That way she could ask him about his health.

Jackie placed the flowers in a large juice pitcher; she didn't have a vase big enough, then finished laying her clothes out for work.

Everyone was glad to see her, especially Dr. Jefferies. Tracy wanted to know how she liked the party. Jackie said she couldn't wait for her next party just to see if she could out-do herself.

Jackie kept to herself that first day back. She wasn't in a bad mood, just a quiet one. She kept day-dreaming about her few days with Joe and how happy she had been. The inner harmony didn't last long. Monica came to visit Tracy for lunch and talked Jackie into going out with them.

Most of the lunch hour was dedicated to idle chatter. During one of the brief lulls in the conversation Jackie had to ask, "Tracy, weren't you embarrassed going down on Hot Rod at your party?"

"I was so messed up after eating Monica's brownies, and with all I had to drink, and...."

"And as hot and horny as you were," Monica interrupted, "you couldn't wait, could you."

"Man alive, he was big and salty," Tracy grinned.

"Look, Jackie, Monica and I are going night clubbing Friday night, why don't you come along with us? You never know who or what you might catch."

Jackie was happy to be included in their plans. However, she knew that most night clubs have a core of regulars. The kind of men she was after were the out-of-towners. She wasn't looking for a steady, just someone she could get to volunteer pay for services rendered.

"You like to dance?" Monica was asking, but Jackie was barely paying attention.

"Uh, as a matter of fact I do."

"Good, then it's a date, tomorrow after work we can change at my house, go out for the freebies at happy hour, get some studly-like men to buy us drinks, and then dance all night at the Blue Moon Grotto." Monica was making plans.

"What is the Blue Moon Grotto if I may ask?" Jackie said.

"It's an upscale night club where rich guys go. So wear something clingy."

"Tracy," Jackie asked, "aren't you getting married soon?"

"Ya gotta live it up before you give it up," came Tracy's quick reply.

Lunch was over and work was calling. Jackie really didn't want to go. Joe had given her the extra hundred dollars so she really didn't need any extra money.

That night when she laid out her clothes for work the next day, Jackie also laid out a hot pink pant suit with a silk V-neck blouse and her lucky pearls. Jackie still wasn't sure she should go. She never had any female friends, and even though these girls were much younger she liked, the fact that she would be doing things she never did before, was stimulating.

It was a quiet Friday as Fridays go. In fact the last appointment canceled at four. That left no one else for Dr. Jefferies to see, so he closed the office a half hour early that day. Jackie forgot to call Joe.

Tracy drove Jackie over to Monica's apartment. It was a small one-bedroom like Jackie had, except it was in a more exclusive part of town.

"Wow!" said Jackie, "This is nice, how can you afford such a swell place?"

"She sells brownies to supplement her income," Tracy interrupted then laughed loudly.

Tracy wore a sleek khaki outfit complete with hat and boots. Monica wore a denim mini skirt, black fish net stockings and a see-through black blouse. Of course she had her complete array of ear and nose rings.

"Where first?" Tracy asked.

"The Hilton, it's closest and the food is great for happy hour. Is that okay with you, Jackie?"

"I'm just here for the ride, you lead the way."

The three girls jumped into Monica's Volkswagen and took off. The airport Hilton was fifteen minutes down the road and packed. Every Friday was ladies' night with half-price drinks and a great buffet. With so much enticement for the ladies, the men were sure to follow. And they did.

The lounge was so jammed with people they had to stand up to eat and drink. Refills were coming as compliments from guys from all around the bar. Jackie stuck to wine. She had built up a tolerance and could drink more wine than hard alcohol.

Jackie watched with amazement as one man after another came on to Monica. She was equally amazed at how deftly she avoided their clutches and how sadistically she taunted them. She would kiss each one, hug them and rub her crotch on their legs, then laugh, turn away and ignore them.

The air was thick with smoke, and noise; the room reflected the pandemonium of the participants. At the buffet table the three girls filled their plates to overflowing several times.

Someone offered Jackie a cigarette, she took it. She wasn't a smoker, but she subscribed to the theory, "When in Rome...."

"I've got to go, want to come with me?" Monica asked. Tracy nodded yes so Jackie said, "Sure, why not."

They had to wait for several minutes to get an empty stall. Jackie, who wasn't used to smoking, complained about a headache. Monica reminded her the night was very young and offered her a small blue pill.

"What is it?" asked Jackie.

"It will help you get through the noise and smoke," Monica answered.

Jackie thought it must be some sort of Excederin and took it. The girls emptied their bladders and returned to the bar.

The noise, the people all talking to and ignoring one another at the same time amazed Jackie. Her head was swimming with confusion. She started to lose her balance, Tracy grabbed her elbow and caught her just in time.

"You okay, Jackie?"

"Yeah, just a little, I don't know what..., the ground just seemed to disappear."

"She'll be all right, I gave her something to calm her down," chimed in Monica.

"Aw, shit," snapped back Tracy, "what'd you go and do that for? I told you not to mess with her tonight."

"OK, OK, OK!"

"Let's blow this joint." Tracy was directing her conversation to Monica, "Jackie should come down on the way to the Blue Moon Grotto."

The trio took off with Jackie sitting in the back seat singing to herself; having the time of her life.

The three got out at the entrance to the Blue Moon Grotto and the parking lot attendant took off with Monica's trusty steed.

There was a large waterfall at the entrance spilling into a lava lake with large goldfish and flowering lily ponds. The girls walked up the short flight of stairs to the circular bar overlooking the two dance floors. There were D.J.'s at each end rotating during breaks and strobe lights with mirrored globes every fifteen feet or so.

Illuminated cages with nearly nude beautiful women lined the perimeter. The color theme was shades of blue and lavender. The place was exceptional. Jackie had only seen lounges like this in movies. Her jaw dropped wide open when she saw the full design from above.

"Come on, Jackie." Tracy was still leading. "Let's sit down for awhile and catch our breath."

The girls sat at a booth-like table on the third level above the dance floor. Tracy and Monica ordered exotic mixed drinks and Jackie a large diet coke.

Tracy and Monica left for the dance floor before the drinks arrived. Jackie was asked to dance twice by some handsome patrons but declined, citing a migraine headache. Jackie's head was still spinning. She didn't completely understand what was happening, but common sense prevailed and told her to sit tight.

"Did you see? Did you see that hunk that asked me to dance?" Tracy asked Jackie.

Jackie smiled, she wanted to speak but her mouth wouldn't work.

Monica broke in, "That guy in the blue blazer had a hard-on before we hit the dance floor."

The three laughed and giggled like school girls on their first night out. Eventually Jackie got up and danced with the friend of the man Monica was dancing with and teasing unashamedly. Monica kept fondling her breasts and rubbing her crotch. When her dance partner would grab for her she would blow him a kiss and slide just out of grasp.

There were more free drink offers than the girls could handle. Half-filled cocktail glasses rimmed their table. Some of them had been drunk, some spilled, others just appeared.

The tempo of the evening suddenly took a terrible turn with the inclusion of an uninvited guest.

"What the fuck are you up to?" Robert, Tracy's fiancee, suddenly appeared in front of the table.

"Hey, Robbie, baby." Monica tried to make light of the situation.

"Shut the fuck up, Monica. I expect the only reason Tracy's here is because of you."

Jackie sat speechless. Robert was a tall, blond football player type. Sitting down as Jackie was, and looking up, he seemed even taller and more dominating. His fury scared her.

Robert grabbed Tracy by her wrist and began pulling her from the booth.

"Ouch, you're hurting me, let go!"

"Hey, buddy, you heard the lady, let her go!"

The guy Tracy had been dancing with tried being gallant and intervening on her behalf. Robert wasn't interested. He was almost a foot taller than his opponent. He let go of Tracy's wrist and smashed the man in his face.

The room erupted into screaming and cursing and crying. It didn't take long for the bouncers to get to the disturbance and break it up. They threw everyone out. Tracy and Robert were still fighting in the parking lot when the attendant brought Robert his car.

"I think I'd better go home with Robert," Tracy told Monica, "we need to work this out. Will you see to it that Jackie gets home okay?"

"Yeah, sure I will. Are you going to be all right? I'll call the cops now if you want," Monica added.

Tracy was crying. Robert was honking his horn and the attendant was pleading for her to get in and quit making a scene.

Jackie got in the front seat of the V.W. and Monica headed her relic towards home. The man Monica had been dancing with, and his friend, the man Tracy had been dancing with and Robert punched, got into their own car and followed behind. The two girls, filled with booze and drugs, didn't notice.

Thirty minutes later Monica pulled her car to the curb in front of her apartment. She and Jackie got out and headed up the stairs. The two men following pulled up right behind them.

"Hey, Monica, you got to help my friend, his nose is broken and he's bleeding all over the place."

"Take him to the hospital," Monica shouted from the top step.

The two men huddled for a few seconds, "All right, but let us come in and get some ice for his bloody nose."

Monica, too drunk to think straight said, "Oh, all right, come on in."

Jackie didn't have an opinion. Her world was moving much too fast.

Once inside Monica's apartment, Jake, the guy who had been dancing with Monica, went to the kitchen for ice, while Tommy, the guy Robert punched, sat on a kitchen stool trying to stop the nosebleed. For whatever reason, Monica disappeared to the bedroom with Jake leaving Jackie to play nurse to Tommy. With his head back Tommy reached up and grabbed Jackie by her breasts.

"What? Stop that! You've got to go now."

"You want it. I know you want it. All your kind does."

Tommy stood up grabbing Jackie by her wrists and pushed her backwards into the living room. Jackie tripped on the carpet and fell to the floor with Tommy landing on top of her. He started nuzzling her neck, bloody nose and all.

"Stop it!" Jackie shouted and tried to scratch him.

"Oh, a wild cat, huh. I like feisty women."

Tommy grabbed Jackie's blouse and ripped it open, scattering buttons all around. Jackie managed to free one hand and tried to slap Tommy's face. Instead she missed but her hand nicked Tommy's nose causing him to scream in pain. He responded by slapping Jackie hard in the face.

"So the bitch wants to play rough, huh." He slapped her again and finished ripping off her blouse. Jackie was kicking and crying. Tommy reached back and slapped her so hard the ring on his hand cut her cheek.

Temporarily stunned, Jackie stopped fighting. Tommy took it as a sign of submission and tore off her slacks. That act revived Jackie's disgust and she

153

began screaming, slapping and scratching; Tommy punched Jackie in the face breaking two teeth and knocking her out.

Monica, wearing only her white lace panties and an opened blouse, came running out of her bedroom.

"Get the hell off of her you son-of-a-bitch!" she yelled and jumped on Tommy's back.

"Get this bitch off of me," yelled Tommy.

Jake followed Monica and pulled her by her hair. While he held her down Tommy punched her in the face and stomach.

"God-damned bitches," Tommy said holding his bleeding nose.

The two men went through the girls purses taking what money they had; Jackie had a lot. They left the women laying unconscious and bleeding on the floor. Sometime later that night Monica was first to regained her strength and was able to help Jackie to the couch. Jackie had a split lip, so Monica wanted to take her to the hospital, but Jackie said no.

Both women had badly bruised faces and blackened eyes. Jackie took the worst beating. By dawn the bleeding and swelling was under control. Jackie and Monica slept all day. Later that evening Monica drove Jackie home; neither spoke.

Jackie called Dr. Jefferies when she got in and explained that she had broken a tooth. She wanted to be seen before hours so she could leave and go home before the office opened for business. She didn't tell Dr. Jefferies how bad it really was. He agreed to see her at seven-thirty.

"My God," said Dr. Jefferies when he saw Jackie. "You need to go to the hospital for X-rays and sutures."

Jackie pleaded with him to just fix her two broken teeth; of course he did. Then he sent her home for a week to rest and recuperate, without pay. She had already used all her sick time up.

When Tracy came in an hour later and saw Jackie she went ballistic.

"My God, what did Monica do to you?" And with that Tracy called Monica and cursed her out. Because Jackie had taken the bus to work as she always did, that morning Tracy got Dr. Jefferies to let her drive Jackie back home. She stopped by the Rite-Aid on the way to fill the prescription Dr. Jefferies had written.

Jackie was in severe pain. She felt as bad as she looked.

"Look, Jackie, I'd have you stay with me until you get better except Robert moved back in last night. He wants to keep an eye on me. So, I feel really bad. Is there anything I can do for you while I'm out?"

"No, thanks, I just want to sleep."

Jackie let herself into her cold, barren apartment. As soon as she finished the routine of locking all the locks, she broke down and cried bitterly.

Later, she went to her refrigerator, there was no orange juice, and she had no cash and little money in her checking account. Thoughts of suicide began to enter her head. The reality of the moment was hitting her.

14   GUILTY CONSCIENCE

The doctor had given Joe a clean bill of health. The police caught the two teenagers that robbed Joe; but they had used the money they had stolen for drugs. Joe felt sorry for the couple, but not sorry enough to drop charges. The girl it turned out was only sixteen, a runaway from Kansas, and her nineteen year old boy friend was also facing charges of contributing to the delinquency of a minor.

First thing that Monday morning, the Monday of Thanksgiving week, Joe took his cab in for an oil change. Joe averaged a thousand miles a week. He tried to change it every three thousand miles, but it was usually closer to four thousand.

On his way back home the radio station was already playing Christmas carols. Joe loved Christmas carols. He could listen to them year around. "Peace on earth, good will towards men" should last all year he thought, not just for one month.

Even though the winter was milder than usual it was still cold. The day time highs were in the upper thirties or lower forties on occasion. The wind chill always made it seem much colder. It was on days like these Joe regretted not having a fire place.

Ever since Martha passed, Joe would go down to the soup kitchen in town at Thanksgiving and volunteer as a server to the underprivileged. It kept Joe from becoming depressed and the next day he would always feel a sense of pride and accomplishment.

Joe passed a Holiday Inn; the marquis boasted of having the largest Thanksgiving day buffet in town for nine dollars and ninety-five cents. Joe thought he might make a change from his usual routine and go out to eat.

He stopped by the cleaners to drop off the coat and pants he had worn the night he took Jackie out; he wanted to make sure they were clean in case he had an occasion to use them again. Next, it was on to the drug store to fill his last prescription.

With Christmas tunes spinning happy thoughts, Joe completed his morning errands and went home to Felix, who, as usual, was standing guard in the bay window.

"Hey, little buddy, did you miss me?"

By the time Joe got in the kitchen Felix was, as usual, standing on the counter next to the door in his capacity of official greeter. The two made each other very happy.

Joe opened his mail and paid some bills. Then he went to his recliner for a nap before going on the late shift. Joe was slowing down with age, and he knew it.

As Joe slept in his recliner, Jackie woke up in her apartment late that same afternoon. It was just before sunset. She went to her kitchen and started a pot of hot water for some tea. While the water boiled, she rummaged around her refrigerator for some food. There was some chicken left from Joe's. Seeing it caused her to stop and reflect. Picking up the dish to put it in the microwave brought tears to her eyes as she recalled the sense of pride the evening had brought her.

The whistle from the tea kettle brought her back to reality. For the longest time Jackie just sat at her table and dipped the ginseng tea-bag up and down, up and down. She sat staring at the steam wondering if people could truly read tea leaves, and if they could, what the future held for her.

After her skimpy meal, Jackie went to the bathroom to run a hot bubble bath. She thought soaking in soft bubbles, and spoiling herself with perfumed water, might just help her feel better.

As the water ran and the foam began to build, Jackie disrobed and for the first time since morning looked at herself in the mirror. What she saw shocked her to tears. Her face was swollen, her cheeks badly bruised, her left cheek was cut, and her eyes blackened. If Jackie had had drugs in her apartment she surely would have overdosed on them. Jackie sat on the small white throw rug in front of the tub and cried until she could cry no more.

The dentist office was closed on Thursday and Friday because of the holiday so she would only miss three days of work. But she needed those three days. She had been robbed as well as beaten. What would she do? She couldn't go to the bars and pick up any men, who would want her? Her depression was having to make room for despair.

While growing up, Jackie had always been a happy girl. Why not? She had always been protected, first by her family, and then by her husband. Jackie's world was always somewhat of a story-book. Now Jackie was faced with the ugliness of reality and the pain of not being in control of her own destiny. As she lay in her tub of hot, foamy water, drowning in self pity, Jackie gave some thought to the idea of returning to church. She had always been religious, but somehow blamed God for her baby having died and Harry abandoning her.

Jackie's body hurt all over. She was sore and in pain. She wanted some wine, but then remembered how free she felt after eating some of Monica's brownies. That would work except she knew deep down she didn't want to get mixed up with drugs. Jackie really didn't want to see Monica again; she didn't trust her.

The phone rang.

Jackie's first impulse was to answer it, but that meant she had to get up from her warm, tension relieving bath. Her need for personal comfort overcame her curiosity. She let it ring.

Jackie had begun her bath by the light of the setting sun. The room was now dark. The small bathroom window that let the light in was now letting in the dark.

Jackie liked the dark. You can hide in the dark, you can't hide in the light. The dark blankets you with secrecy; the light displays your pain and shortcomings.

Quietly she stepped from her bath and stood motionless in the dark as if waiting for inspiration.

The sudsy water dripped down her china white skin and puddled at her feet.

Her heart ached. It was not as a result of her beating. The physical pain she could deal with and she knew in time it would go away. The ache in her heart was more discomforting and real. Jackie sat on the edge of the tub and slowly dried off, waiting for guidance that never came.

Joe called dispatch to let them know he was on duty. Mondays were never busy unless there was something going on downtown which only happened in the summer.

A s Joe drove around town that night he noticed that most of the stores were stringing Christmas lights and fixing their windows with holiday displays.

Joe's first fare that night was an elderly woman who was doing early Christmas shopping. Joe helped her put her bags of gifts in the trunk.

"You know," she said, "the Friday after Thanksgiving is known as black Friday. That's when the shopping season officially kicks off and the stores are jammed. That's why I go on Monday; to beat the crowd."

"I see you have a lot of presents. You must have a large family," Joe remarked as he helped her with her bundles.

"Those are just for my grandchildren. I send my grown kids cards, but little kids like to open presents. Do you have any children?" she asked.

"Just Felix," Joe replied with a smile, "he's my buddy, a genuine thoroughbred alley cat."

The two chatted about pets and kids. The evening got off to a good start.

On Mondays, Joe would take a dinner break around nine-thirty at a little pub called 'Pauley's.' Joe always ordered a Reuben on rye with a cream soda and watch thirty minutes of Monday night football. Joe played high school football, and he enjoyed watching the pros play.

The football game that night was boring. Joe got to thinking he hadn't heard from Jackie for almost a week. He thought for sure she would have at least called to thank him for the flowers or to see how he was doing.

He decided to drive by her place and drop in. It was almost ten. He argued with himself that it was too late. He lost the argument. He went to see her.

Joe decided to drive around the block first. He was nervous. He had butterflies. He kept telling himself it was too late, but he just wanted to see Jackie. Finally he pulled up to her building and knocked at her door. After he knocked he was petrified. He didn't know what he was going to say, or why he was there. He hoped she wouldn't answer, although he knocked again, but not as loud.

Jackie had been in her bed doing cross-word puzzles when she heard the sound of a door knock. She slipped on a robe and went to the peep-hole and peered out.

"Oh, my God, no!" Jackie thought to herself. A part of her was excited and wanted to open the door, the rest of her was ashamed and wanted to run and hide.

Jackie didn't have to make a decision, Joe made it for her. He decided she must be asleep and left.

Jackie panicked as he turned to leave. She wanted to open the door and yell, "Joe, don't leave, I need you. Joe, please come and take care of me."

Instead she turned, rested her back on the door, put her hands to her face and cried. As she cried she slid to a sculptured pose on the floor. "Joe, oh, Joe," she repeated between sobs.

The next morning Jackie found the message Joe had stuck in her door:

"Dear Jackie,

I called, but you weren't home. I tried visiting you between fares but, I guess I came by too late and you were already asleep. I wanted to know if you would like to have Thanksgiving dinner with me at one of those fancy 'all you can eat' buffets. Please call. Joe."

Jackie had been crying all night. But when she read the note, she cried once again. Jackie was touched by Joe's thoughtfulness. She didn't want him to see her as she was so she decided not to call, and if it ever came up why, she could say the note must have blown off or someone had stolen it.

That next day, Tuesday, Joe busied himself with some shopping of his own. He hadn't had a Christmas tree since Martha passed. While he was waiting to get his prescription filled the day before, he had noticed a display of two-foot tall fake Christmas trees complete with lights, ornaments, and an angel on top. Joe bought it. For whatever reason, he wasn't sure why, he felt revitalized and as young-at-heart as ever.

He placed the tree in the middle of the bay window and plugged it in. The lights twinkled and Joe grinned from ear to ear. Felix smelled it and decided it was not a threat.

"Look, Felix, the angel looks just like Jackie." He wondered if she had gotten his note, and if she did, why hadn't she called?

It was getting late and Joe had to go to work soon so he decided to call her at the dentist office where she worked.

"Happy Holidays, Dr. Jefferies' office," Tracy answered the phone.

"Yes, ma'am, I'd like to talk to Jackie Jones, this is her friend Joe."

Tracy hesitated, "I'm sorry, sir, but Jackie is off today." Tracy felt an anxiety attack coming on.

"What time does she come in tomorrow?" Joe demanded.

"I'm sorry, sir, but Jackie won't be in for the rest of the week. Can someone else help you?"

"This is Joe, I'm a good friend of hers, I want to know where she is."

Tracy knew about Joe. Jackie had talked highly of him during their breaks and over lunch. She didn't want Joe to make a scene and she didn't want to get Jackie in trouble either.

"Look, Joe...."

"I demand to speak to Dr. Jefferies," Joe butted in. Tracy decided to come clean and try and soften the blow.

"Joe, Jackie is at home, she wasn't feeling well when she came in on Monday, so she took the rest of the week off."

Joe slammed the receiver down, and without saying good-bye to Felix took off out the door. He was worried, very worried. He had called her the day before and she didn't answer the phone. What if she was so sick she couldn't?

He drove directly to her apartment building and ran up the steps. He began banging loudly on her door.

"Jackie, are you all right? Open up Jackie, it's me, Joe. I'm not leaving until I talk to you."

Joe hesitated for as long as he could, which wasn't very long, and began beating on the door again. He stopped when he heard the sound of opening locks. Jackie opened the door, but kept the chain lock on, so the door would only open a few inches. She was wearing her robe and stood back from the door so Joe couldn't get a good look at her.

"What do you want?" her voice was impersonal and strained.

"What in the blazes is the matter? They said you are sick. I called and you didn't answer. I was worried." Joe was really worried because Jackie wouldn't let him in. That wasn't like her.

"I'm coming down with the flu and I don't want you to catch it. Thank you for coming by, but please, let me go get some rest now."

Joe knew instinctively something was wrong. "Please, let me in. Do you need medicine or anything?"

"I'm fine," and Jackie shut the door.

Joe heard her fasten the locks, causing him to leave with a heavy heart.

Jackie went to her room and cried the rest of the evening. Joe went home heart-sick. He was sick to his stomach with grief. This woman he barely knew had come into his life and turned it upside down.

Wednesday was the busiest day of the year. He was constantly taking people to the train station or to the airport. Joe was too busy to worry about Jackie. Holiday travelers are usually in a good mood leaving, and therefore good tippers. Joe did very well.

It was almost ten that night when Joe pulled into his driveway. He had been on the go since seven that morning with only time out for gas and coffee. He was tired, hungry, and had a terrible back ache.

He said hello to Felix and went right to the shower. After washing off the road grime of the day he rummaged through the refrigerator and took out a home made TV dinner Jackie had made for him and popped it in the microwave.

Joe stood up in the kitchen and ate the meal from the counter top. He was too hungry to be formal, and too tired from sitting all day.

"Come on, Felix, tell me about your day."

Joe picked up Felix and headed to his recliner. There the two slept until morning. When Joe turned to the 'Today Show' they were showing Macy's Thanksgiving Day Parade.

Joe was depressed. He felt old for the first time in years. He didn't want to get up. If it hadn't been for nature's call he would have stayed in his chair feeling sorry for himself. Just as he started to sit down again a commercial came on TV advertising a buffet for Thanksgiving dinner, no reservations needed.

Joe knew just where the restaurant was; he called and asked if they had carry out; they said yes. Joe asked them to prepare a complete meal for him including dessert and he was on his way down to pick it up.

Joe left his motor running while he ran in and picked up his food. Then he placed the large good smelling bag of fresh cooked food on the seat next to him so he could be sure it wouldn't spill. The aroma made Joe hungry.

Then Joe headed for Jackie's apartment. He knocked on her door, she either wasn't home or wouldn't answer. "Jackie, I hope you're home, I'm leaving you a package by your front door. Please take it inside so it doesn't get cold. Oh, yeah, and Jackie, if you feel like talking, gimme a call."

As Joe turned to leave he heard the chains rattle on the door locks. He didn't turn around. He didn't wait.

15   A REAL THANKSGIVING

Joe drove home like a madman. He was both angry and hurt. He thought it rude the way Jackie was treating him, after all the nice things he had done for her. As he cooled off somewhat he remembered the good things she had done for him in return. That caused conflict in his heart and mind, the conflict brought a hurt he hadn't known for years.

Joe was headed for home when he realized how upset he was and that he didn't want to go home and yell at Felix. Joe was very even tempered, but when his emotions got away from him he knew it was best not to be around people.

Joe drove around for hours. He wasn't wearing his cabby's uniform and he had the sign on top of his cab turned to "Off Duty."

He decided to drive downtown and look at the lights and the pretty window displays, thinking that would help cheer him up. He found a radio station that was just playing Christmas music so he turned it up really loud and sang along.

Joe was stopped at a red light when he was startled by someone banging loudly on the passenger side window. Joe turned to see a stocky man in a three piece suit holding a briefcase. He rolled down the window, "Sorry, mister, I'm off duty."

"Please, please," the man entreated, "I need a ride to my home. Dinner has started and I'm the guest of honor."

Joe didn't have anything better to do so he turned the radio off and let the man in.

"Where to?"

"Thank you, thank-you, sir, the rectory of St. Christopher on Fairmont street."

"I know where it is. How did you get to be caught downtown on a holiday?"

"I'm the president of the bank and each year our bank holds it's annual Thanksgiving Day dinner for the orphanage. Each year after dinner I pass out envelopes containing fifty dollars for each orphan to do his or her Christmas shopping. This year I forgot and left them in my desk drawer. I hurried down to get them but when I came back out of the bank my car wouldn't start. Thank God you just happened by."

"Wow!" said Joe, "That's some story."

"How come you're not with you're family?" the gentleman asked Joe after catching his breath.

"My wife, Martha, died some years ago, so I usually go to the soup kitchen and help serve meals, but this year I got sidetracked and didn't make it."

Joe pulled up to the rectory.

"How much is the fare?" the banker asked.

"Naw, that's okay, you just have a nice holiday. I think what you're doing for the kids is really something special."

The man held out twenty dollars to Joe, "At least let me pay for your gas."

"No, really, I'm glad I could contribute."

"I'll make a deal with you, I'll put this twenty dollars towards the orphanage if you'll have dinner with us. There is plenty of food, and if you hadn't stopped, the children would have been very disappointed."

Joe thought about it for a few seconds, and knowing he had nothing better to do, said, "Sure, why not."

The phone rang at Joe's house. On the fourth ring the answering machine picked up, "Hello, I'm not home, Felix is but he can't answer the phone so leave a message."

Jackie listened to the entire message. She missed the sound of Joe's voice. When she heard the beep, she hung up. In a way she was glad Joe wasn't home; she really didn't know what to say.

Her small kitchen table was filled with food, more food than she could eat in one sitting. "My God," she thought, "isn't he a caring person."

Joe was a simple man, unpretentious, and what you saw was what you got.

"Kind, thoughtful, loving, honest," Jackie was listing all of Joe's attributes, "and not wanting something in return. I've never met a man like him before." The more Jackie thought about Joe the more depressed she became until she broke down and cried.

Jackie picked at her food. Even though she was hungry, she knew she didn't deserve the thoughtfulness Joe had shown her. There was a large slice of southern pecan pie for dessert. One of Jackie's favorite's. There was another small bag inside the big bag from the restaurant. It came from the drug store where Joe had filled his prescription. Inside it was a new book of cross word puzzles and a get well card.

"Why is this man doing this for me? Why is he treating me this way? Why doesn't he just leave me alone?" Jackie was shouting at the ceiling as she sobbed. Jackie was acting like a lot of people. She didn't know how to handle sincere warmth and generosity.

Joe sat at the head of the long table with the banker and the monsignor. The monsignor gave thanks and everyone bowed their heads; "...and thank you, Lord, for sending Joe to us this day, he was truly God-sent in our time of need."

"Amen!"

Joe's face turned as red as the cranberry sauce. After the dessert, when everyone was filled with good food and fellowship, the children came to Joe one at a time and thanked him personally for being a modern-day good Samaritan.

After dinner everyone retired to the rec. room and the mother-superior played Christmas carols on the piano. Joe sang along too. Everyone had such a good time. Joe was sad when it was finally time to say good-bye to all his new friends.

Perhaps I'll see you in church Sunday, Joe," said the monsignor as he shook Joe's hand good-bye.

"That goes double for me," said the banker.

Joe left with the children waving good-bye to him. He couldn't remember another day in his life when he was so happy or so fulfilled.

Jackie finished wrapping all the food she didn't eat and put it in the refrigerator or the freezer compartment. She washed and dried the dishes, and then put them away. As she was cleaning up she thought about Joe and Felix. She thought how much she needed to call and say "thank you." Jackie had drunk the nectar of depression and was intoxicated by it.

In a cry for help she called Joe again, hoping the machine would pick up. She had worked up enough courage to leave a message; she couldn't talk to him in person.

After the beep, Jackie stammered "Hello, Joe, I uh, wanted to...," She fought to keep her voice from breaking, "I mean, the food was great, and, uh, I..., you're a good man, Joe. I've never known any better." And with that Jackie hung up and cried once again.

It was getting late in the day, the sun was setting. For many people when the sun sets so does their will power to fight.

There was a storm approaching and the winds blew hard.

Joe parked his cab and ran to the kitchen door to keep from getting blown away.

"Gees, Felix, did you see that? The wind is really blowing out there."

Felix jumped into Joe's arms and licked him under his chin.

"Cut that out, Felix, you know that tickles."

Joe carried Felix into the living room and over to his recliner.

"Let's see if the football game is still on, okay little buddy?"

Joe sat back, put his feet up and reached for the TV remote which he kept on top of the answering machine. It was then he noticed the red light blinking, signaling him that he had a message.

Joe got very few messages. During the day he was usually home and answered the phone; at night his few friends knew to call him at the cab company. They would take his messages and then call him on his two way radio.

"Look, Felix, somebody called. How about that."

Joe hit the play button and listened to the message from Jackie. The sounds in her voice troubled him greatly. Joe rewound the message and played it again, then again.

His first impulse was to drive over there and see what was going on, but he decided to call first.

Jackie answered on the fifth ring. She picked up the phone and waited several seconds before saying "Hello."

"Jackie, it's me Joe, I'm on my way over. When I get there I want you to let me in." Joe didn't say good-bye or anything else. He just hung up, put his leather jacket back on and left.

All the way over to Jackie's house Joe fought with himself as to what he should say to her. He wanted to demand that she tell him what was going on. He knew he didn't have that right. At first Joe got really mad that he even had to go over there, then good sense regained control. He didn't have to go over there. She hadn't asked him. He had invited himself.

Jackie was still wearing her robe. At first she thought of getting dressed, but didn't have the energy, or the desire. She did go to the bathroom mirror and tried to fix her hair. There wasn't much she could do about the black eyes, even though they were much better and the swelling had gone down.

Jackie heard Joe knocking at the door, she opened it. Jackie had only the small kitchen light on, making it somewhat dark in the room. Not dark enough to hide the bruises.

"My God in heaven! Jackie, what happened to you?"

"Can I get you a glass of juice or a cup of tea?" Jackie answered Joe's question with one of her own.

"No, no thank you, I'm fine." Joe's voice trembled.

"At first I was going to tell you I fell down the stairs, or got in a car crash or something. But then I decided to just tell you the truth and say good-bye and thanks for being such a good person."

"What do you mean good-bye, are you leaving?"

"No, but you will after you hear my horrible truth." Joe sat down on the stiff wooden chair and swallowed hard.

Jackie didn't tell Joe everything, it wasn't necessary. What she told Joe was that sometimes she found herself short of funds on rent day and had to do special favors for men in order to break even. "But then you offered me a part time job, Joe, and that was a big help." Jackie didn't want to sound unappreciative.

She continued her story from Tracy's bridal shower. She made sure Joe understood she had nothing to do with the night they went out to the

Blue Moon Grotto. That part was painfully true. Jackie had been in the wrong place at the right time. As Jackie described the beating she took she broke down in tears and couldn't finish.

Joe filled up with tears listening to her pain. Finally, he got up, went over to Jackie and put his hands on her shoulders.

"Jackie, I've heard enough, please listen to what I have to say and don't argue."

Jackie continued to sob.

Joe put his hand on her shoulder, "I want you to get some clothes and get dressed. I'm taking you home with me."

Jackie sat up and put her hand on Joe's. She didn't say anything but got up and disappeared into her bedroom. A few minutes later she reappeared in jeans and a sloppy sweatshirt. She had a small over-night bag and a coat.

Joe carried her bag and she followed him to his cab.

"I'll drive," he told Jackie and smiled.

Jackie sobbed quietly all the way back to Joe's. Joe had a lot to say and a lot of questions to ask, but decided his best course of action was silent support.

Jackie was a pitiful sight; her cheeks discolored and her eyes red from crying. She blew her nose and tried to smile. Jackie was a brave woman, foolish at times, but brave.

Joe parked the cab in his driveway, "You stay put and I'll come around and open the door."

"Okay, thanks."

Joe held the door open and then held her by her elbow as they ran to the kitchen door.

The first thing Jackie did when she got inside was pick up Felix.

"Hello, Felix, old friend, it's good to see you again. Did you miss me?"

Joe took Jackie's things to the guest room while Jackie stroked Felix.

"Why don't you take a hot shower and put the robe on, I'll heat you up some soup, maybe you'll feel better."

"Thanks, Joe, I will." Jackie put Felix down and headed for the shower.

Martha used to tell Joe chicken soup could heal anything. So he opened a can and placed it in a microwave dish and heated it up. He set the table and poured himself and Jackie each a tall glass of orange juice.

Jackie was in the bathroom for a good half of an hour. When she came out she had put a lot of face make-up on and was able to hide many of the bruises. Her hair was combed and she was wearing Martha's old robe.

"I thought you might have drowned in there, I was beginning to get worried."

"No, no such luck. Ooh, chicken soup, my favorite."

"You would have said that no matter what kind of soup I fixed."

Jackie just smiled and held her juice glass up, "I want to make a toast to the nicest man I know."

Joe was embarrassed, but toasted her back.

Neither spoke during the meal. Afterwards, Jackie told Joe she was in charge of cleaning the dishes. Joe didn't argue. Joe and Felix went to watch TV.

It was early evening, the sun had set and the wind was starting to slow down just a bit. Jackie came out of the kitchen and sat on the sofa.

"Joe."

"Ya, Jackie."

"Today is Thanksgiving, you went out of your way to try and make sure I had a happy Thanksgiving day. It was my fault I didn't. But I just wanted you to know, it turned out just great thanks to you. I'm really tired, if you don't mind, I think I'll go to bed." Jackie got up and kissed Joe on his forehead.

"Good night Jackie."

Jackie left Joe and Felix watching the tube, it was their throne. About a half of an hour went by and Joe heard Jackie call out.

He got up and went to her room and knocked on the door.

"Come in, Joe."

Jackie was sobbing.

"What's the matter, Jackie?" Joe walked over to the bed.

"Hold me, Joe, I need to be held. Please?"

Joe sat down on the edge of the bed, Jackie, trembling, leaned over and grabbed Joe around his waist. Joe stroked her hair gently. The next morning Joe was still holding Jackie, from under the covers.

16 LOVE OR SEX

The next morning found Jackie sleeping in the middle of the bed facing the wall and Joe right behind her with his arm around her waist. Jackie's robe lay one side of the double bed and Joe's clothes on the other.

Jackie woke up first. She was smiling and felt an inner peace she hadn't known for many years. She grabbed Joe's strong hand and held it tight to her.
Joe began to stir.

Jackie rolled over so she could face him when he opened his eyes.

Joe coughed once then twice and smacked his lips trying to wake up. When he managed to get the sleep out of his eyes he saw the still bruised but smiling face of Jackie greeting him from his slumber.

"Good morning, Joe," Jackie said with a song in her voice.

As if in a dream Joe woke up quickly and pulled back from her hug.

"What's the matter, Joe?"

Joe looked horrified and did a terrible job trying to cover it up.

"Don't you dare," Jackie scolded.

Joe froze and looked somewhat confused.

"Don't you dare pull away from me, Joe. What happened last night was between two consenting adults. There is no sin in that, so don't make one up." Joe was at a loss for words. Jackie wasn't.

"If you try to apologize I swear I'll never speak to you again. Don't cheapen a precious moment."

"I, uh...," Joe tried to speak but the words got lost somewhere between his voice box and his mouth. Jackie turned away from Joe and faced the wall.

"Go ahead, get up and leave me. That's what you want, isn't it?" She was speaking to the wall.

Several seconds went by before Joe answered. "Well no, I mean, I, I just don't want you to think less of me, that's all."

"Look, Joe, I asked you to hold me last night, there's nothing wrong with that. What happened after that came naturally when two people share feeling for one another. You do have feelings towards me, don't you?"

"Why, yes, of course I do," said Joe still talking to Jackie's back.

Then it started to sink in. He rolled towards Jackie and pulled her to himself and gave her a big bear hug. Jackie smiled and slid back into his arms. She grabbed his hand and kissed it.

"Oh, Joe, I don't think you're done with your chores yet." Jackie reached behind her and patted Joe just below his belly.

Joe rolled Jackie over on her back and began caressing her. Jackie lay submissive to his touch and accepted his sensuous advances with pleasure.

Eventually Jackie got up first and took a quick shower. Joe took his after Jackie did, even though she invited him in to wash her back.

While Joe showered and shaved Jackie cooked hot cakes and eggs for breakfast. Not knowing how he liked his eggs, she scrambled them. Jackie was so happy she sang to Felix as she cooked.

She set the table and poured the juice as the coffee percolated. It was a happy house.

Joe sat at the table and waited for Jackie without turning on the television. That was a first for him. Felix was busy licking spoons and helping Jackie. He didn't even bother to greet Joe. That was another first.

"Well," said Joe, as Jackie brought the last of the breakfast items and placed them on the table, "Felix seems to like you as much as I do. The vote is unanimous. We would like you to stay."

Even though Jackie had thoughts of staying on her own, hearing Joe say it set her back. She fumbled for words.

"Look, Joe, lets eat before the food gets cold. We can talk later."

Joe had been around for a long time and knew that was a put off. He didn't like it at all.

"Look, Jackie, maybe you're right. I thought we were getting along better than most people. I even thought there were some special feelings between us.

I apologize for speaking out of turn. I hold special feelings for you, I shouldn't speak for you. Please pass the syrup."

"Here you go," said Jackie as she passed the syrup. "I never asked you to find a place for me in your house or your heart. I'm not a stray that you brought home to feed and release. Please pass the salt."

"Salt is bad for your blood pressure," said Joe. "It's strange that you would refer to yourself as a stray. I would prefer to think of you as someone who took a wrong turn and got lost, if only briefly. A smart person stops and asks directions. That doesn't make the person giving the directions a better person than the person who is lost, only a better positioned one. Please pass the ketchup."

"Ketchup? I didn't put any ketchup on the table. What do you need ketchup for?"

"My eggs."

"Eggs? Nobody puts ketchup on scrambled eggs."

"I do."

"Are you doing that just to upset me?"

"No, I've been putting ketchup on my eggs all my life. Why not?"

"Well, well..., because, that's why not." Jackie's voice showed concern and irritation.

Joe laughed out loud.

"What's so funny? Are you making fun of me?"

"No, not at all. I think we're having our first fight that's all."

Jackie stopped being aggravated long enough to think about what had just happened and laughed with Joe.

"You weren't really serious about ketchup for your scrambled eggs, were you? You just said that to tick me off, didn't you?"

"Nope," said Joe as he got up and went to the kitchen to retrieve the ketchup. He sat back down and poured a small amount right on top of his eggs.

"Ugh! You're not going to eat that are you?"

"Yep!" and he did.

Jackie sat with her mouth open and watched.

"If it bothers you that much I guess you'll just have to cook my eggs over easy from now on. I don't put ketchup on them."

Jackie finished her breakfast and refilled their cups with fresh hot coffee.

"I don't want to quit work," Jackie said point blank.

"I don't want you to quit work either," said Joe. "It's important that you have your own money so you won't feel dependent on me. The house is paid for; all that's left is the utilities and what little food I, or should I say, we, eat."

Jackie sat very still and then began to sob.

Joe sat up straight and began to apologize for whatever he had said that she found offensive.

"No, Joe, it's not you, I, I'm just happy. I'm confused, and I'm scared. Please don't think you've done anything wrong, cause you haven't." Jackie mixed words with tears. "My luck with men, and life in general lately has been terrible. I don't want to make any mistakes, that's all."

"You can't make a mistake if you don't take some action. Doing nothing is definitely a mistake. If you must fail, fail while attempting to reach your goal."

Joe got up and walked around the table. He put his hands on Jackie's shoulders and began to rub them. She made the sounds of a woman being diffused.

"Look, Jackie, stay where you are. Don't make the move on my behalf. You know your situation as it is, if it's what you want, or if it's what you're comfortable dealing with, then don't change a thing."

With that bit of advice Joe went to his recliner and turned on the TV.

Jackie sat at the table wanting to cry. She could not. The pain of despair and the fear of failure were gripping her. She had thought of being a part of Joe's family ever since her first visit. She was having trouble understanding the attraction. Was Joe a life-line in a sea of failure? Was she attracted to Joe because of security? She had not known security since Harry left. Perhaps she was attracted to Joe because of his stable life. Hers had not been stable for a long time now. Perhaps she was attracted to Joe because he was a kind and gentle man. The men she had known recently were neither of those. Perhaps she was attracted to Joe because of the love he had for his wife. She envied that. Harry never adored her like Joe adored Martha. Perhaps she was attracted to Joe because of the order he had in his life. Her life was anything but orderly.

What did Joe need her for? Sex? Joe was a passionate man, a caring man, no not sex. He could hire a maid service to keep his house clean. Companionship? She was still an attractive, articulate woman. Money? Hah, not the pitiful take-home pay she made. Children? Not likely, Joe had the opportunity earlier in life and for whatever reason chose not to have any.

Love? Love had never been mentioned. What about love? The love Joe displayed for his departed wife was admirable. Was love necessary for a relationship to work? Did she love Joe? What was love? Was it a burning desire to share sexual fantasies? Did Joe love her?

The more she tried to figure it out the more confusing the situation became.

She thought about her apartment. She had some good furniture she had kept from her marriage, but other than that, and her clothes, there wasn't anything she wanted to keep, and nothing she would miss.

Still Jackie fought a sinking, hollow feeling. What was it? Joe was sitting quietly with Felix asleep on his lap watching TV. Normally, this time of the morning she would be sleeping it off. Which did she want? Which did she need? More important, which could she be faithful to?

Jackie felt she needed answers. She had a need to know. Recently she didn't care. Now she did. Was she looking for a way out? Was she looking for a reason to turn Joe down? Was she out to self-destruct? God help her.

Felix jumped up on her lap and meowed.

"What's the matter, Felix, is Joe ignoring you?"

Jackie got up, went to her room and got dressed. Then she went to the living room and told Joe to take her home.

"What for? Did you forget something?"

"No, Joe, I just want to go home."

"Did I say something out of line? I'm sorry if I did." Joe's voice strained, his face lost it's color.

"It's nothing you did, Joe, I just want to go home. Please."

"Sure." Joe got up and put his shoes on. He was obviously hurt and confused.

All the way back to Jackie's apartment Joe was on the verge of tears. Jackie couldn't help but to notice. She didn't want to say anything. Anything she might say would only make the situation worse.

When Joe pulled up to Jackie's apartment he didn't open her door; she let herself out. "I'll call you later," she said.

Joe broke down in tears as he pulled away. Jackie didn't look back. She couldn't handle the guilt.

Once inside her apartment Jackie turned on the radio. She found a station that played classical music and turned it up. She purposely left the lights off. She poured herself a glass of juice and went to the sofa in her small living room and sat staring at the closed curtain.

Inside Jackie wanted to cry. She was crying but there were no tears. She had sent Joe away without an explanation. She didn't have a clue as to why. She just knew she had to escape.

"Escape," she thought to herself. "Just what do you mean escape? You weren't held hostage. You weren't being beaten. You were there because a kind man was concerned about your well-being."

Jackie felt her world caving in on her. She was looking for excuses, but excuses for what? For saying 'no' to Joe? For not wanting to improve her living conditions? For not wanting to improve her life?

She looked around her small apartment and knew this wasn't where she wanted to spend the rest of her life.

"Think, woman, think." She yelled out loud. Jackie got up and walked around the small room pulling at her hair and biting her lip.

"Shit, shit, shit." Jackie wasn't prone to curse, but the level of frustration was too much.

She sat down in the middle of the floor in the darkened room and grabbed her knees with both arms. She sat that way for hours without moving. It was like a form of meditation or confinement. Without knowing it, what Jackie needed was to escape into her own world. She needed to get away from the influence of others; especially Joe. Even though he wasn't putting pressure on her directly, just the fact that she was in his domain made her feel restricted in her actions.

Jackie got up and went to the bathroom, still with the lights out, and started a bubble bath. As the water slowly filled the tub and perfume filled the air she looked at her undressed body in the mirror. She compressed her breasts checking for lumps. Her face was healing nicely although her spirit was still showing the scars.

With the tub full, Jackie slipped silently under the sudsy bubbles up to her neck. Jackie liked the water as hot as she could stand it.

Did she love Joe? The question was paramount on her mind.

"Let's skip love for a second," Jackie began a conversation with herself. She thought if she thought out loud it might help her to understand.

"Do I like Joe? Yes," that question was easy.

"Do I care about Joe? Yes," another easy question. "Do I want Joe to like me? Hmm, I think it's obvious he already does, but do I like it? Yes, he makes me feel like a woman inside, without making me feel threatened."

Finally after ruling everything out, she asked herself the core question: "What about his age, does it bother me?"

A tear slipped from her eye and rolled down her freshly scrubbed cheek.

"Yes!"

Joe was almost twenty years older than Jackie. He didn't look his age; his hair had very little gray and he was in good physical condition. She was worried about what her friends would say. She was worried that her friends would accuse her of finding a father figure and not a husband. "A husband, that's it, a husband," Jackie shouted out loud and jumped out of the tub sloshing water everywhere.

Her wet, naked body ran to the phone, "Joe, I need to see you right away, please don't ask me anything over the phone, I'll explain when I see you, and Joe, please drive carefully, I care about you." She hung up and got dressed.

17   MAY/DECEMBER
HAVE NEVER BEEN CLOSER

Jackie turned the lights on, looked around her small unpretentious apartment and turned them back off. When Joe knocked, Jackie was sitting in the dark with only the night- light from the kitchen to see by.

"Did you forget to pay the electric Bill?" Joe joked, trying to break the ice.

"No, Joe, I didn't forget to pay the electric bill." Jackie took Joe by his hand and led him to the sofa. She sat him down on one end, and sat facing him on the other.

"Joe, I've got a lot of things to say, I'm nervous, and I don't want to cry. Please don't say anything until I'm finished."

"Do I need a good stiff drink of whiskey?" Joe tried to make a joke.

"It's not funny. Please."

Joe turned, put one leg on the sofa and faced her.

"Joe, this morning at breakfast you said you wanted me to stay."

"Yes, and I meant it too."

"Please, Joe, don't interrupt."

"I'm sorry."

"Anyway," Jackie continued, "it is a big step. It's a step I'm willing to take, but I don't want to jump into anything. I know you care for me Joe, it's evident the way you act and everything. But you're nice to everyone; I don't want to be an 'everyone', Joe.

"I want to be loved, I want to be held and told I'm pretty even when I'm not. I want someone to like the woman inside of me as well as the person outside.

"I want to be number one to someone. I can't begin to tell you how much I admire your Martha. She was the luckiest woman on earth. She had your love and I'm sure you had hers.

"Joe, there's a lot of pain in this world. You can't protect me from it anymore than I can protect you from it. I don't want to hurt anymore, Joe, I'm tired of hurting. If I stay here my pain is contained. It won't get any worse, or better, I know what to expect. If I go to your house who knows what will happen.

"I don't like who I am, Joe, because I don't like my station in life. I think I am a better person than the one you know. I hurt deep down inside, Joe, it's a kind of hurt band-aids can't help. I don't like what I seem to be becoming or the direction I appear to be going. I'm scared, really scared.

"I don't want to move in with you to run away from the reality of my situation. I don't want to move in with you to keep from facing the responsibilities of my actions. I still have to own up to the things I do.

"I want a man who will love me deeply, hold me tight, and make all the bad things in life seem worthless. But I want a man I can love without the fear of rejection. I want a man who's not so macho he won't let me hold him when he's hurting. I want to return love, not just reflect it.

"I want a man who will know how to be tender and know when I need physical love as well as emotional love. I want a man who won't reject me when I tell him I need those things.

"I want a man who will let me share the burden, not divide it up into pieces and distribute it out. I'm not afraid to do my part. I'm not afraid to sacrifice for the good of the team. I don't want to be the sacrifice.

"Joe, right now I'm afraid to love you, but I want desperately to love you. In fact, it hurts deep down inside when I deny myself the pleasure of loving you. I'm just scared, that's all."

Jackie had taken Joe's shoe off and was massaging his foot while she was talking. So far she hadn't cried although she had come close. She hesitated.

"I'm almost done.

"If I do move in with you, Joe, it's on the condition that you make an honest woman of me. I won't rush you, I just want your word that you will."
Joe had put his other foot on the couch and Jackie had began to work on it while she spoke.

"I don't want to compromise your virtues," Joe spoke quietly. "I don't want you to do anything you don't want to do.

"As far as love goes, I'll be honest with you. I don't suppose I'll love another woman like I loved Martha. She was unique. Our love grew as the years passed, she was special. I have a lot of love to give; giving it makes me feel better inside. If I give love and it's not returned, that's okay, I don't love just to be loved back. But I must admit, when you do love someone and they don't love you back it is embarrassing.

"Jackie, since the first time I met you at Green's Deli I felt something deep within me stir. At first I just figured it was old age, but the more our paths crossed the stronger the feeling grew. I do care for you, I care very much. How much care does one need to call it love? I don't know.

"I would like to take care of you because of the care I feel inside. I don't want to take care of everyone I meet.

"I don't want to know who you were, I want to learn who you are. I would like you to consider these things while you make up your mind."

Jackie had quit rubbing Joe's feet and was sitting quietly crying a soft cry. She put Joe's feet down, crawled across the couch, held his face in her hands and kissed him gently.

After a few minutes of kissing, Joe said, "Come on Jackie, get your bag, we can continue this at home."

"Your home," said Jackie, disrupting the moment.

"No, our home, if you'd like."

Joe took Jackie back home and the two shared a shower and a bed that night.

Sunday morning Joe told Jackie he would like to go to church and asked her if she would like to go with him. She said she had been meaning to return to church for some time now and this would be a great opportunity to start over fresh.

Joe and Jackie got up early that morning and took care getting dressed.

"Where are we going to church?" Jackie asked.

"St. Christopher's, that's where I spent Thanksgiving dinner with the orphans, remember?"

Jackie looked as lovely as she looked nervous. Joe was handsome, and the couple looked as if they were made for each other.

The two decided to sit in the rear of the church in case either one of them felt uncomfortable and wanted to sneak out. That didn't happen, and the beautiful cathedral added to their religious experience.

At the end of the service the monsignor and the altar servers walked down the center isle to the back of the church. He always greeted the parishioners as they exited the service.

Joe and Jackie sat and enjoyed the peace and harmony offered by their surroundings. When the crowd had significantly dwindled, Joe and Jackie left.

They stood in line to meet the monsignor.

"Good morning, Joe," the monsignor said as he saw Joe approach, "I see you didn't forget where the church was. I hope you had a wonderful Thanksgiving."

"I did, monsignor, I want you to meet my fiancee, Jackie."

Jackie's mouth dropped open.

"Your fiancee, how wonderful!" he reached out and shook her hand. "Remember we celebrate weddings, too. Remember us when you're ready."

"We will, monsignor, thank you," said Joe.

"God bless you both."

Joe and Jackie walked fifteen or twenty feet down the cobblestone walk when Jackie stopped and turned to Joe.

"Your fiancee?" she said, trembling, as she held both of his hands.

"Yes, that is if you'll have me. I got to thinking, if I make an honest woman out of you then you can make an honest man out of me, deal?"

"Oh, Joe, it's a deal."

Jackie jumped up and hugged Joe around his neck, crying happy tears.

"You're going to get me to start crying if you don't stop," he said.

"Who cares. I better not hear anyone call you a cry-baby or they'll have to deal with me," Jackie said still hugging Joe.

"Come on," said Joe, "let's go break the news to Felix."